No More Heroes

David W. Palmer

Dreamviu Publishing

No More Heroes
A Dreamviu Publishing Trade Paperback Book

Published by Dreamviu Publishing
Livermore, California

ISBN-13: 978-0-615-36139-0
ISBN-10: 0-615-36139-0

Dedicated to the
creative futures of Bob and Katie
and the
creative legacy of Kurt.

Chapter 1
(The Beginning)

The hero of our story, Chase Hancock, was average in pretty much every way, except one. He was born in a nondescript town in a nondescript state in the midwestern region of the good old U.S. of A. About the most interesting thing that happened to him in his early youth was that he stuck his mother's keys in an electric outlet.

It's not interesting that he did that, per se, because kids stick things in things all the time. The interesting thing is that he didn't electrocute himself. He had the good fortune to stick a key into the ground side of the outlet first and that the keys were on a ring that took most of the juice when he stuck the second key in. It did give him quite a jolt, though, and knocked him hard on his young little ass. He's pretty sure that's when he started remembering things.

Chapter 2
(The Future)

"Wait," said Kurt, looking across the polished chrome kitchen table at his father. "Maybe you shouldn't start quite so far back. I can only stay until about three o'clock."

"Okay," his father answered, happy that his son would be visiting for another couple of hours, remembering how much he loved having him around. "The fact is, there's not a whole lot more to tell until Mr. Hancock was in college. I don't know much more, anyway. As far as I know, he had a pretty normal mid-western upbringing. He went to school, he lettered in wrestling, he went to church, he and his father liked to hunt. You know, pretty much normal stuff for back then. Why are you interested in this guy, anyway? He was only a minor figure in the run-up to the Catalyst. As I'm sure you remember from high school, Dr. Randal Howard was the central pre-Catalyst figure."

"Someone left me a short note that had Chase Hancock's name on it."

If Kurt had been paying more attention, he would have seen his father's face lose a shade or two of color. For most of Kurt's life, his father had worried that something like this might happen. And now apparently it had. "What kind of note, what did it say?" Kurt's father asked slowly.

"It was just a note, Dad. It wasn't a big deal. When I saw the name, though, I thought of you because I know you've spent a lot of time studying this guy. So, go on, please." Kurt's tone of voice sounded more like an order than a request.

Kurt's father ignored his son's tone and said, "Wait, if we're going to be here a couple of hours, there's something I need to do. I'll be back in a minute." Kurt's father got up and went toward the bedrooms.

Kurt hadn't spent much time in his parents' house lately; or, more correctly, in his father's house since his mother didn't live there anymore. As he waited for his father, he looked around the kitchen and marveled at how little things had changed over the years; not only over the years since he was a boy, but over the years in general. There was a lot of chrome and glass in his father's house, in a post-Catalyst neo-modern style that had been popular when the house was built. There were highlights of red and burnt orange here and there added as a misguided reminder of sunrises and sunsets that ended up being mildly nauseating, rather like the avocado colored appliances of a bygone generation.

But there was still a sink, refrigerator, microwave, and electric stove in the kitchen (electric because gas was expensive enough that only people at the highest levels could still afford it). There had been a period when many 'kitchens' didn't have all the normal appliances because people rarely had time to cook. But now that people had time to do more than worry, work, sleep, and shit, they did a lot more cooking at home. There had also been a time when refrigerators had shrunk to a size small enough to keep beer, white wine, and ice cream and not a lot more. That's when virtually all food had been vacuum-packed and irradiated, meaning that it could be stored at room temperature. But then as people thought about it, they realized that eating is one of the deep pleasures of life and that a New York strip steak out of a plastic bag just isn't the same as one straight off the blade of a butcher's knife.

There were still beds in the bedrooms; sinks, toilets, and showers in the bathrooms; and chairs, couches, and flat-panel displays in the living rooms. The car Kurt had driven over in still had four wheels and a steering wheel, just like the first one that rolled off Henry Ford's assembly line in 1913. It ran on hydrogen rather than fossil fuels, though, and had anti-collision technology and other features that Henry Ford wouldn't have thought of even in his wildest dreams. The car illustrated two of the three technological things that had changed the most in the last fifty years or so: renewable energy and computers. The third was communications.

There had also been dramatic advances in human biology. Most (but not all) diseases had been cured or controlled. Organ re-growth and replacement had been perfected – except the pesky old brain. The pesky old brain had eluded controlled re-growth and successful transplant and in a way people weren't upset about that. People weren't upset about that because they were realizing that immortality probably wasn't all it was cracked up to be. After all, how many times can you find new joy in visiting Paris, or Rome, or Athens, or London, or New York? A hundred? A thousand? A million? Probably less than a million...

Most of the dramatic advances in human biology had been on the inside. On the outside, people looked pretty much as they had for thousands of years. There had been a blending slowly but surely taking place, though. Most racial and geographic barriers had been knocked down, meaning that inter-racial coupling had become common. This had the interesting and slightly ironic effect of blurring racial distinctions. The blackest black wasn't quite so black any more and the whitest white wasn't quite so white.

Kurt, himself, was a product of just such a coupling. His father was clearly of European descent, with brown eyes, slightly graying brown hair (grey hair was still on the human biology fixit list), about 6 feet, 2 inches in height (about average, in other words), and average build. Kurt's mother was a very attractive woman of African descent. Kurt leaned toward his mother in looks, with light brown skin, dark brown eyes, and nearly black, slightly kinky hair. Kurt had attractive, slightly rounded facial features and a muscular build. Kurt's parents had stayed together a couple of years after their coupling contract expired when he turned

21, but then had decided to go their separate ways. They were still good friends.

Kurt's nostalgic thoughts were interrupted by his father coming back into the kitchen. "It's about time," Kurt said. Kurt's father ignored his son's remark and went on with his story.

Chapter 3
(The Present)

The first time Chase saw Lacey was in the library at UCLA. As she walked in, he (along with most of the young men and, frankly, most of the young women) gazed at her, trying not to blatantly stare. She had a very feminine and equally unnecessary light-pink bra translucing through her slightly cut-off tank top. Not just a little of her matching panty peeked out over the thin waist of her shorts that were pulled down slightly on the left side. Chase figured this wasn't on purpose, because she didn't seem like *that* kind of girl. He got the sense that it wasn't sloppiness, either, but rather a casual, confident nonchalance that he found particularly attractive, partly because it's something he'd been striving for for years with only occasional and usually short-lived success. As he gazed, Lacey caught his eye and, to his surprise and mild distress, didn't let it go. She had vivid blue-diamond eyes, her face was set in short but stylishly cut golden hair. Her nose was slightly too big; but all that did was make her a 9.8 rather than a 10. She sat down at the half-height cubicle directly across from Chase. He was still gazing... and so was she.

He expected that, if she were going to say anything at all, it would be something like, "*Nice day, isn't it?*" So, her first words caught him a little off guard. Respecting the semi-quiet of the library, she whispered, "I don't quite understand why matter has mass."

Chase doubted that he'd have much luck with, *"Let's get out of here and go someplace where we can talk more easily."* So, he tried to whisper as best he could that according to the Standard model of physics, there's a fundamental particle called the Higgs boson that gives matter its mass.

"No," she whispered, "I didn't say, 'I don't quite understand *how* matter has mass', and I pretty much get the Standard model. I said, 'I don't quite understand *why* matter has mass'."

"Oh. Well, I guess that's just how God made it," Chase said without really thinking about it very much.

"Gee, and I thought everybody says you're brilliant," Lacey said a little louder than she needed to. Chase glanced around to see who heard that.

"Well, I guess everybody's wrong," Chase whispered.

Lacey gave a little smile. "Let's get out of here and go someplace where we can talk more easily," she said.

"Well... okay," Chase said, nearly dropping his laptop on the floor as he fumbled it into his backpack – so much for casual, confident nonchalance.

As she stood up to leave, Lacey straightened out her shorts. Okay, so maybe she was *that* kind of girl.

Chase wasn't sure any more. Whatever the case, he was flattered to have her attention and most of him desperately wanted that to be enough. But, despite her recent jab at him, he actually was pretty brilliant and that part of him forced its way through and wondered why she would give a 7.5 like him even a second glance, much less seek him out and ensnare him with her tantalizing questions and light-pink panties (either one of which alone would have had no trouble working). He also wondered who the hell she was.

As they got into the hall, Chase said, "You know, I'm pretty sure I'd remember if I'd seen you around before. Did you just transfer in or something?"

"No, I don't go here," Lacey answered.

"Well then, what..." he paused, confused.

"Have you heard of Professor Howard?" she asked.

"Yeah, I've heard of him. I've never had him, but some of my friends have. He was just in the news recently, wasn't he? He was speaking at a rally criticizing our status quo or something like that, right? The truth is, I didn't really pay much attention."

"That's right. He was speaking at a rally. He's been getting himself into some pretty deep stuff. But I'm getting ahead of myself. Anyway, he should be in the news again. But he isn't."

"Why should he be in the news again?" Chase asked.

"He's in the hospital. He's close to death," Lacey answered with a bit of strain escaping through her otherwise controlled voice.

"Oh, I'm sorry to hear that," said Chase. "But, unfortunately, lots of people are in the hospital near death. Most of them aren't in the news."

"How many have been poisoned by a Pinky?" Lacey asked.

"A Pinky?" Chase said incredulously. "Come on, Pinky's are an urban legend! They're not real. How come you know so much about this Professor Howard, anyway?"

"Because he's my father. My name is Lacey Howard."

"Oh, nice to meet you," Chase said automatically. "My name is – Oh wait," Chase said, interrupting himself as what Lacey had just said sunk in. "I'm really sorry to hear about your father."

"Thanks," said Lacey. By this time, they had walked outside and were approaching a parking garage.

"Wait, are we going somewhere in particular?" Chase asked.

"I'm not sure if we are or not. Would you mind taking a ride with me?"

Again, most of Chase desperately wanted to go. "Well, I'd really like to. But —"

Lacey interrupted, "Come on, Chase, do I really look like someone you should be worried about?"

"No, I guess not. Okay, let's go. I guess I shouldn't be surprised that you know my name, by the way."

"No I guess you shouldn't," Lacey said as they walked into the parking garage and toward her BMW.

Chapter 4
(The Present)

Lacey drove to an older, more run-down part of town and then into the parking lot of a hospital that Chase wasn't familiar with. She parked in guest parking.

"Are we going to see your father?" Chase asked.

"Yes," Lacey answered.

"Why isn't he at the Medical Center?" Chase asked, referring to UCLA's first-rate medical facility.

"I'm not totally sure," answered Lacey. "He started there. But they said there was something about his case that could be handled better here. They also said the security was better here, whatever that means. Maybe they suspect he was poisoned, too. But if so they haven't done anything about it, like call the cops."

"So, what do they say is wrong with him?" Chase asked.

"Acute liver failure; like possibly a result of heavy drinking, they said. I don't think they believe me when I tell them he doesn't drink very much. But he doesn't. Anyway, I can't get anything more out of them."

"Can't your mother get more information?"

"My mother's dead. She was killed in a car crash about 10 years ago."

"Oh, I'm sorry," said Chase.

"It's okay," said Lacey. "It was a long time ago."

As they entered the hospital, Chase was struck by how old it looked. It didn't seem dirty or dilapidated, just old. Chair rail molding surrounded a small lobby area. The walls were dark brown below the molding and nearly white above it. The floor was well-used hardwood and the ceiling, trimmed with an ornate crown molding, was the same nearly-white color as the upper part of the walls. A woman as old as the hospital or older was sitting at an ornate information desk. She nodded at Lacey with a slight smile, as though Lacey's face was a familiar one to her. As they walked toward the elevator, Chase looked down a hall and saw that it had the same décor as the lobby, except that the floor was a marbled brown and gray linoleum rather than hardwood. The doors looked like paneled wood with doorknobs you turn rather than metal with the rectangular things you push.

Chase and Lacey took the elevator up to the second floor. The hall they came out on looked the same as the one Chase had seen on first floor. They walked by a security guard at the entrance of the Intensive Care Unit and checked in with the nurses at the central desk. The ICU looked much more modern than the rest of the hospital so far. There were several sliding glass doors surrounding the central desk that opened into single rooms filled with machines with dials and buttons and monitors and gauges and beeps. All of the rooms had some combination of cards, flowers, balloons, pictures, and/or drawings made by five-year-olds, except one. Lacey led Chase through the sliding glass door of that one – her father's room.

As they walked in, Chase observed that Dr. Howard was a middle-aged man, probably in his early 50s. He had graying brown hair and a neatly trimmed beard. He had oxygen in his nose and an IV in his arm. "What happened to his hand?" Chase whispered. There was a stub between Dr. Howard's left elbow and where his left hand should have been.

"He lost it at the very end of the Vietnam War," Lacey whispered back. "He really doesn't like to talk about it, so I'm not sure of the details. He was reaching out to keep a friend from stepping on a landmine, but it was too late. His friend, unfortunately for him, caught most of the shrapnel. But my father caught some too, and his hand got infected. That's about all I know."

"Hi, Dad," Lacey said, taking her father's right hand. There was no response.

"He's been unconscious almost the whole time he's been here," Lacey said. "About three weeks ago, he stirred a little bit. But that's been it."

"Dad, I brought Chase Hancock with me." Lacey thought she felt a nearly imperceptible squeeze on her hand, but she wasn't sure. "Dad, can you wake up? Chase wants to talk to you." Chase looked at her as if to say, "*I do?*"

"Dad, come on, wake up." There was no response. "Damn. I was hoping having you here would have some effect."

"I'm sorry, Lacey, but why on earth would my being here make even the slightest difference to your father?" Chase asked.

"When my father became semi-conscious about three weeks ago, I was here. He whispered five and only five seemingly random words to me: 'pinky', 'poison', 'chase', 'hancock', and 'bomb'. Since then, I've been doing a lot of research. From what I've found, I'm nearly certain that a Pinky poisoned my father and I think there's a severe bomb threat."

"Okay, so why don't you do something about it?" Chase asked.

"Okay, so why don't you help me?" Lacey answered.

Although Chase could name every element on the periodic table, along with atomic weights and common isotopes, interpersonal-related things sometimes eluded him. He was finally starting to get this interpersonal-related thing, but not totally. "Lacey, have you taken a look at me? I'm not exactly the kind of guy who can handle rough-and-tumble bad guys with bombs!"

As a matter of fact, she had taken a look at him. She had seen a lean, average height, reasonably muscular body. The reasonable muscles were probably from occasional workouts that were probably a throw-back to his high school wrestling days. *Old habits die hard,* she thought. She had seen dark brown hair with a short Super Cuts cut. She had seen black full-framed glasses with rounded-corner rectangular lenses that didn't completely uncompliment a strong-featured face. She had seen the only thing that normally might have made her to take a second look at Chase: deep set piercing brown eyes with lighter and darker brown filaments that shot randomly and unevenly out from his pupils; the kind of eyes that hinted at a strength of character that was becoming harder and harder to find these days; the kind of eyes that had an intriguing depth that could draw a girl in and possibly not let her go if she wasn't careful.

"Yeah, I see what you mean," Lacey answered. Chase grimaced a little bit, but more on the inside than the outside. Lacey didn't notice. "I've been thinking about that a lot," she continued. "Let's not talk about it here, though."

"Goodbye, Daddy," Lacey said, turning her attention back to her father and squeezing his hand. There was no response.

Chapter 5
(The Present)

"Let's take a walk," Lacey said as they left the hospital. "Let me get a jacket, though. It's getting kind of chilly out here." As she said this, Lacey noticed that the sun had gone down while she and Chase were in with her father. They went to her car and she slipped on a pair of sweatpants that were in her back seat and a sweatshirt. "There, that'll do," she said.

As they started to walk, Lacey said, "So, like I said before, I've been doing quite a bit of research. As far as I can tell, the Pinky legend is true. Pinkies seem to be the most cunning, creative, ruthless killers on the planet, ever. They're bionic and there are at least 2 of them."

Chase looked at Lacey. Until then, she seemed like a rational, reasonable person. Now he wasn't so sure. "I think the stress of your father may be clouding your thinking," he said, trying to say, "*I think you might be crazy*," as nicely as he could.

"Listen," Lacey said sharply, knowing she might be sounding a little deranged but not happy that Chase was thinking it, "my father is a very intense, focused man. It's actually scary sometimes. So, why would he choose the word 'Pinky' to be one of the 5 words he could say to me, possibly for a long time, possibly forever?"

"How am I supposed to know?" Chase answered. "Maybe his pinky hurt."

Realizing she wasn't likely to make much progress going in this direction, Lacey changed the subject. "Okay, believe what you want to believe," she said. "Like you said earlier, you're not exactly the right guy to be battling bad guys. So, you must be the right guy to be battling bombs."

"But I don't know anything about bombs," Chase objected.

"Oh, really? What's TNT?" Lacey asked off-handedly, like she might be asking the time.

"Oh, that's just short for trinitrotoluene. It's a pale yellow solid that forms in crystals and ends up being a powerful explosive. It's made of nitrogen, hydrogen, carbon, and oxygen. I could write down the chemical formula for you, if you want —"

"No thanks, Einstein," said Lacey, interrupting Chase and thinking to herself, *Jeese, is this guy for real?*

"Okay, I get your point," said Chase. "I'm not a complete idiot. But there's a huge difference between knowing what might be in a bomb and actually finding a bomb or being able to do anything about it. I've never actually touched one, you know." (*Well, not counting the three or four I made when I was a kid, until I blew the back off my garage and my father wouldn't let me do it any more,* he thought to himself.)

"Oh, really," said Lacey. "What about the three or four you made when you were a kid, until you blew the back off your garage and your father wouldn't let you do it any more?"

"How in the *hell* did you know about that?" Chase asked. (Chase didn't use words stronger than 'heck' and 'darn' very often. But there were exceptions.)

"I have my sources," Lacey answered. (Which, in this case, was a local newspaper article she found on the Internet when she Googled "Chase Hancock". But she didn't bother mentioning that.) "Anyway," she went on, "you're a pretty smart guy, right? And what are you smartest in?" Chase smiled a little bit, but more on the inside than the outside. Lacey didn't notice.

"I don't know," Chase answered. "I guess computers. That's my major, anyway."

"And where do you find most things, or at least start looking for most things, these days?"

"I guess computers," Chase answered.

"Yeah," Lacey said.

Chapter 6
(The Present)

Chase hadn't been paying much attention to where they were walking and, apparently, neither had Lacey. When he did pay attention, he said, "You know, this isn't exactly the best neighborhood to be walking around in at night."

As if on cue, three rough looking characters stepped out from an alley a few feet in front of Chase and Lacey and turned to face them. All three of them had semi-long sloppily-kept black hair, the kind you might expect to see a bug crawl out of at any moment. They all had black leather jackets on; but if they didn't, purple track marks would have been obvious up and down their arms. The tallest and skinniest of the three had a noticeable scar down his left cheek. He also had his hand in his pocket and was poking it forward, as though he was pointing a gun. "Good evening, folks," he said with mock friendliness, as though he were welcoming not really wanted guests into his home for dinner. "I hope you're having a nice night. I'm afraid my boys and I are going to have to put a bit of a damper on it, though. Just be cool and you won't get hurt. Now, just take out all your money and all your jewelry and put it down there on the street in front of you. Okay?"

Lacey cursed herself for being so God-damned stupid. But she wasn't sure what to do. Was there really a gun in that pocket, or just a fist with a pointed finger? Chase, for his part, just stood there frozen. Lacey decided not to take a chance and said, "Okay, how about everything but my watch. My father gave it to me and he's in the hospital. He may die."

"Ah, I'm really sorry to hear that... But that is a real nice looking watch. Now, take the mother fucking thing off and put it down on the street! Now!" he yelled. All hints of mock friendliness were gone.

One of the other rough looking characters, who was comically too round for his leather jacket, was looking at Lacey, but not at her watch. "You know, Jack, she's a pretty fine looking woman."

"Yeah, she is, now, isn't she, Harry? In fact, now that you mentioned it, she might just be too fine a woman to take just money and a crumby old watch from. Why don't you boys go hold onto Mr. Dickshit over there," he said, taking his gun out of his pocket and pointing it at Chase, "while I get to know Miss America a little better. Or is it Ms. America? I can never keep that kind of thing straight these days."

Harry and the other rough looking character went over and grabbed each of Chase's arms and pulled him away from Lacey. "Now hold on real tight, boys. I don't want Mr. Dickshit getting overly excited when his woman and me start hitting it off real good. You know, as I'm giving her the pleasure he can only give her in his wet sticky dreams and she starts moaning and groaning and buckin' around all crazy like, he might just try to break free to see just how I'm doin' it. Course, even if he sees, it won't make a bit a difference with the little pin prick I'm sure he's got."

Jack moved toward Lacey and she tensed up as he brushed the muzzle of his gun across her neck as he walked behind her. With his gun in her back, he petted her hair like he was petting a kitten. "Kind of short, but it's nice and soft, baby. Jesus, I'm getting hard just touching your hair. Let's see, what can I touch next? Oh, by the way, in case you didn't hear, my name's Jack. That's so you know what to scream out when you're cummin'. Either that or 'oh my God, oh my God.' I'll leave that up to you. And that's Franky over there, and the fat one's Harry. That's so you can scream out their names when they're fucking you too, okay?" He pushed his gun into her back a little harder.

Jack glanced over as a car approached. But the car just drove by with the driver either oblivious to what was going on, too afraid to do anything about it, or probably a little of both. Lacey tensed up more as Jack moved his hand down her left arm and cupped her left breast. "Look, guys," he said, "I'm her living bra!"

Franky and Harry sniggered and one of them said, "Yeah, but that's only half a bra. Come on, do the other half, too, do the other tit..."

Jack hesitated for a moment, but then decided Lacey wasn't much to worry about. "Okay," he said to Lacey, "now, don't move, baby. Just stay nice and still there for a minute, okay?" Jack stuck his gun in his belt and started moving his right hand up to cup her right breast. That was a mistake.

Feeling Jack's right hand on her body without a gun in it, Lacey stretched her arm fully forward and brought her elbow back hard into Jack's ribs, breaking his grip. In what looked like a single fluid motion, she spun around and brought her knee hard into Jack's balls. The sharp pain shooting up his body made Jack buckle over. Lacey knew that was enough. But even so, as Jack folded forward cupping his crotch, she raised her hands over her head, laced her fingers together, and slammed them down hard on the back of his head. She knew she didn't kill him. But there wasn't any sense missing the chance to make him think twice about trying to forcibly fuck the next Ms. America who happened by, right?

Seeing Lacey make her move, Chase wrenched his arm free from Harry's grasp, pulled himself forward a little, and delivered a sharp uppercut to Franky's solar plexus, crashing him to the ground gasping for air. He swung the same fist around like a hammer and hit Harry's nose, snapping it cleanly and making blood spurt profusely. Chase didn't know it, but a slightly more direct hit would have driven Harry's nose into his brain and killed him. Chase tackled him to the ground for good measure, which actually wasn't very hard. As Chase got up and the adrenaline wore off just a bit, he was actually kind of surprised at what he had just done.

"How in the heck did you know how to do that?" Chase asked Lacey who was pulling Jack's gun out of his belt. As she slipped the gun into her sweatshirt pocket, she paid more attention to Franky and Harry. Like Jack, they were lying on the ground, broken, bleeding, and gasping for air.

"Fifteen years of Taekwondo – third-degree black belt," she said, putting her hands together and giving a slight bow.

Chase instinctively returned the bow. "My wrestling coach made us take Karate, mostly for balance and flexibility. I think he liked the spiritual part of it, too, although he never said anything about it. I don't think –"

"Chase," Lacey said sharply.

"What?" Chase said.

"A little more information than I really need right now!" Harry was holding his nose and making moves like he might be getting up. Franky seemed to be getting his breath back, too.

"Oh, right. Okay, so I kept it up, so six years of Karate – brown belt."

"I know," Lacey said.

"How do you know that? What else do you know about me? I suppose you know what underpants I wear?"

"Tighty-whiteys, 34 inch waste," Lacey guessed.

"How the heck?" Chase was actually starting to get a little worried. "Maybe we should get out of here," he said.

"Gee, you think?" Lacey said sarcastically.

They started walking back to Lacey's car – quickly.

Chapter 7
(The Past)

Lacey was wrong about Pinkies, but not as wrong as Chase. There *were* Pinkies and they *were* the most cunning, creative, ruthless killers on the planet, ever. But they were only partly bionic. In fact, they weren't that bionic at all, really. They were given a bionic eye that could see very close and very far away and had night vision. They were given a bionic ear that could hear very quiet things and very far away things and frequencies way beyond a human ear, even beyond a dog's ear. And they were given an internal radio that fed into their other ear to receive orders and other information. But that was pretty much it.

The problem with adding these bionic devices was that, at the time Pinky technology was developed, it was easier to connect signals *into* a human brain than *out of* a human brain. The reason was that pathways into the brain were known, like the optic nerve for the bionic eye. But unused pathways out of the brain were not known. So, there was no easy way to set up a control path for the bionic devices so the Pinkies could, for example, zoom their bionic eyes in and out or tune their intracranial radios.

To solve this, the part of the brain that would normally control a Pinky's left little finger was disconnected from the nerves going to the little finger and used to control the bionic devices instead. So that the left pinky wouldn't be completely useless and so it wouldn't just stick out all the time, the left ring finger nerves were connected to the left pinky as well. The only downside of this, of course, was that the left pinky couldn't be moved independently. This didn't really affect much other than playing the piano and typing. And, the fact is, Pinkies didn't spend a whole lot of time playing the piano or typing. With training, the use of the pinky nerves to control the bionic devices was remarkably effective.

Lacey also wasn't right about the number. There was a total of five Pinkies, not two. A new Pinky was recruited and trained every ten years, or so. Pinkies were recruited young, usually from the teenage runaway population. The pool of teenage runaways was larger than most Americans realized as they lived their sometimes happy but often oblivious lives, giving the Pinky program an abundant supply of possibilities. A small team of recruiters would observe runaway populations and then scrutinize the most likely candidates for months to assure that the best and the brightest were found. And since some of the best and the brightest teenagers in the country were unfortunate enough to find their ways onto the streets, the Pinky program was able to recruit some of the highest quality teenagers in America, bar none.

The mastermind of the Pinky program had a sense of humor, if not necessarily the creativity to go along with it. It made sense to him to name his first recruit

Pinky and then he simply went through the finger names for the rest of them. So, over the years the Pinkies were named, from oldest to youngest: Pinky, Ringo, Fuckfinger, Index, and Thumbelina. To distinguish him from the Pinky program, itself, Pinky was commonly known as Pinky Prime or simply as Primo. Fuckfinger was almost always known as Fred (for obvious reasons). Index was also known as Dex. Thumbelina's more common name was Lena. Lena was the first and only female recruit, but also the most ruthless by some people's estimation.

At least at the beginning, Pinkies didn't know who other Pinkies were. One exception to this was that Ringo knew who Primo was, because he had to kill him. The reason was that Primo had a high-profile world changing kill that started to eat away at him. He performed the kill flawlessly – in fact, to this day, despite considerable investigation, people still don't know what really happened. But the kill started him thinking, which is a very bad thing for Pinkies to do, and he started to develop a conscience. (In Primo's defense, training hadn't quite been perfected yet when he was recruited.) It got to the point that he was making noises about going public. In fact he started doing that in a tentative way. That's the only reason that anyone outside the Pinky organization knew even the slightest thing about Pinkies and that was the beginning of the Pinky legend. So, Ringo got the message to take Primo out over his bionic intracranial radio receiver and that's what he did. Knowing who he was dealing with, Ringo expected the kill to be a tough one. So he sabotaged a plane that he knew Primo would be on. There was some collateral damage – 109 people, including pilots and crew, to be exact. Pinkies almost always tried to avoid collateral damage. But there were exceptions and this was one of them. The authorities determined the crash to be equipment failure.

Besides Primo, all other Pinkies were alive. At least that's what most people in the Pinky organization thought. Many of them couldn't be completely sure, though, because a few years after killing Primo, Ringo went off the grid and hadn't been heard from since (at least that's what many people thought).

Chapter 8
(The Past)

The Pinkies were controlled by the Pinky Control Agency, appropriately enough. It might seem a little brazen to put the name of the super-secret Pinkies in the agency name. But it didn't matter because the Pinky Control Agency went by the acronym PCA and only a handful of people knew what PCA stood for. The handful of people did not include the President or any members of Congress who might actually have been interested in what they were funding. In fact, the President and members of Congress who might actually be interested in what they were funding didn't even know the acronym, because it was rolled up into another budget line item called Internal Presidential Protection (IPP) in the Secret Service budget. Nobody in Congress really knew exactly what the IPP did. But everybody agrees that presidential protection was important. So, as long as that line item didn't go over a few hundred million dollars a year, nobody bothered caring.

The last person who did bother caring, an eager young Congressman from Minnesota who was generally an upstanding individual with a genuine concern for his constituency and country and who thought he might start making his mark by trimming some fat off the federal budget, ran into a patch of bad luck. He was at a cocktail party supporting Ducks Unlimited when a drop-dead gorgeous woman showed a subtly aggressive interest in him. After a drink or two too many, he found himself in a place neither he nor his wife nor his children nor his constituents nor his church would ever have expected him to be: in bed between the drop-dead gorgeous woman's widely spread legs. Although both he and the drop-dead gorgeous woman agreed that this was a mistake and vowed never to speak of it again, somehow the press found out.

When confronted with a remarkably detailed description of his one night indiscretion, the young Congressman readily admitted it and offered a heartfelt apology to his family and his constituents. Unfortunately for him, in the news business forgiveness is generally left to the God of Jesus and Mary, particularly during a slow news week. So, the young Congressman's heart-felt apology didn't matter. The press relentlessly ran the story of his "illicit affair", including every excruciatingly unnecessary aspect of it, down to the décor of the hotel room he and the drop-dead gorgeous woman had 'fornicated' in. Finally, the young Congressman had to resign in disgrace and found himself in another place he never would have expected to be: without his wife or his children or his constituents or his church.

Although the press never got more than the drop-dead gorgeous woman's first name, Lena, she too was apparently in disgrace, because she was never seen nor heard from again. A rumor circulated a few months later that a pregnant woman matching her description had crossed the border into Mexico. But that rumor was never substantiated and probably wasn't true. The young Congressman's successor had no interest in the IPP budgetary line item.

The PCA, as part of the IPP, started innocently enough as an organization to neutralize immediate threats to the president. But in a relatively short time, the phrase "immediate threat" was interpreted more and more broadly until eventually it covered virtually any perceived threat to the American way of life or, more correctly, to the power structure that controlled and profited most from the American way of life. As time went by, the beneficiaries of the PCA's services became long and included many politicians, many prominent corporations, and even a popular movie star or two who were considered important to America. Of course virtually none of these beneficiaries were aware that they owed a debt to the PCA because, as has been previously mentioned, only a handful of people knew that the PCA even existed.

The slide of "immediate threat" from *actual immediate threat* down the slippery slope to *virtually any perceived threat to the American way of life or, more correctly, to the power structure that controlled and profited most from the American way of life*, was made easier by the precursor of the PCA. The precursor of the PCA was originally formed to save the president of the time from an embarrassing actress who was showing him far too much affection. Ironically, a little over a year later, the precursor of the PCA was used against that president himself.

Chapter 9
(The Present)

Chase didn't sleep very well the night of the mugging and attempted forcible fucking. After Lacey dropped him off, he spent a couple of hours pacing around his living room, trying to burn off residual adrenalin and relax a little bit. When he finally gave up and went to bed, he found his mind and body still churning. *Okay, this is normal*, he thought to himself. *Getting mugged at gunpoint tends to have this effect on people.* But he knew that wasn't all of it. A lot of what Lacey had said was swirling through his brain. Was there really a severe bomb threat? Were there really such absurd things as Pinkies? Should he really help her? Or, was she the semi-sane, mostly-delusional daughter of a severe alcoholic? As the exhausting events of the day finally started to win and he finally started to doze off, he resolved that it would be relatively easy to check on Dr. Howard's drinking habits. Then, he would start to know whether to believe Lacey. He really wanted to...

When he woke up from a fitful sleep about three hours later, it was still too early to call anyone who might know Dr. Howard better than he did. So, he logged onto his computer to try to find a way into the L.A. Police Department network. He figured that if Dr. Howard was a heavy drinker, he would likely have a DUI or two under his belt. It took Chase about an hour-and-a-half to find a backdoor into an inadequately protected system behind the LAPD firewall. *Gee, a little slow today,* he thought to himself. *I guess that's what lack of sleep will do to a guy.* From there, it was easy to find Dr. Howard's arrest record. Besides a ticket for rolling through a stop sign about six years before, Dr. Howard seemed as clean as a whistle. *Okay, this is good,* Chase thought.

Next, Chase hopped over to the proprietary patient records on the UCLA Medical Center network. That was easy, because he and a couple of his like-minded friends had hacked into that system several months ago, primarily out of boredom. For grins they thought they'd check out what sexually transmitted diseases their more popular classmates might have had – not that that information would have been of any practical use to them, of course. That turned out to be less fun than they had hoped. In fact, it turned out to be downright depressing. The less fun part was that it seemed like most of the people who slept around, or at least were rumored to sleep around, were careful about wearing condoms, or checking with each other before fucking, or not going to the UCLA Medical Center if they caught something. The downright depressing part was that a classmate who they all liked, but who they thought had flunked out (because she said she was flunking out), actually had late-stage cervical cancer. They didn't look around anymore after that.

Chase looked up Dr. Howard's medical records and found that he followed a relatively normal male doctor-visit schedule – a routine checkup every five years or so. The latest had been about two years ago and there didn't seem to be anything abnormal. There was no mention of alcohol use or any liver problems.

By that time, it was late enough to call other people without too much fear of being shot at the next possible opportunity. So he called Larry, one of the friends who had hacked into the Medical Center with him.

"Hello," Larry answered groggily.

"Hey, Larry, it's Chase."

"Chase, dude, what the fuck time is it?"

"It's 10:30 in the morning," answered Chase.

"Oh, okay. I guess I won't have to shoot you the next time I see you then. What's up?"

"You had Dr. Howard for a class a couple of years ago, right?"

"Yeah, I had him for a Poli Sci elective. Why?"

"How was he?" Chase asked.

"He was okay. Kind of a tough grader. I still aced his course, though, of course," Larry said with a bit of academic pride. "He knew his shit, though. I've got to give him that much. Are you thinking of taking one of his classes?"

"No," Chase answered, brushing off the question. "What about his personality?"

"His personality? What am I, a fucking shrink? What are you asking this stuff for?"

"It's complicated. Come on, help me out, what was the guy like?"

"Okay, well, he was pretty fucking intense," Larry answered. "He had this way of looking at you that made you squirm in your seat just a little bit. I swear, he made a girl cry once."

"He never came to class hung over or anything, did he?"

"That guy? No way! He's straight as a fucking arrow. They say he got his hand shot off in a fucked up bar fight in Vietnam and never touched a drop again," said Larry.

"That's not the way I heard it," said Chase.

"How did you hear it? Come on, what's this about?"

"He's in the hospital, really sick," Chase answered. "I know his daughter. I'm just trying to help her out a little."

"You know his daughter? Since when?"

"A while ago. Not too long ago."

"Alright, dude," said Larry. "For a while there, I was starting to wonder if you even liked women."

"Screw you," said Chase. "It's not like you're exactly Mr. Casanova, you know."

"Screw you, too, fuck-brain. So, the guy's in the hospital, huh? He finally pissed off the wrong people?"

"What do you mean?" Chase asked.

"I haven't paid a huge amount of attention. But I hear he's been making speeches about how fucked up the American financial system is."

"So, that's nothing new. People have been making speeches about that for decades."

"Yeah," Larry said. "The difference is, people are starting to buy into it. Howard's got the have-nots wondering why they actually have not. But that's about all I know."

"Okay, thanks," Chase said, making a mental note to ask Lacey about that.

"So, what are you doing later?" Larry asked.

"I don't know, man, I've got quite a bit of homework."

"Nerd," Larry said.

"Yup.   Right back at ya," Chase answered. "Thanks."

"No worries, dude. Later…"

"Later…" Chase said, hanging up.

Chase called a couple of other people who knew Dr. Howard better than he did and got pretty much the same story. *Okay*, he thought to himself, *so, this is good.*

Chapter 10
(The Present)

Mid-afternoon of the same day (the day after the mugging and attempted rape), Lacey called Chase and he answered. "How are you doing?" she asked. "How'd you sleep after our little adventure last night?"

"Oh, I slept great," Chase lied, partly because he didn't want to admit how much a few little things like getting mugged, seeing her almost get raped, and beating the shit out of three guys freaked the hell out of him and partly because he didn't want to admit that he had spent the better part of the day investigating her father. "I just got up a couple of hours ago."

"Oh, really?" Lacey responded in a not very believing voice. "I pretty much couldn't sleep at all. I dozed here and there, between tossing and turning, but that was about it. That's what getting mugged, almost getting raped, and beating the shit out of three guys will do to a person, I guess... Well, some people, anyway. So, are you going to help me?"

"I haven't really thought about it too much," Chase answered. He didn't usually take quite so much liberty with the truth. He wasn't quite sure why he was doing it now. "How about if I poke around the web a little to see if I can find any leads on a possible bomb threat?"

"That would be great," Lacey said. "And how about, as payment, I bring over some burgers later. Around eight o'clock? Would that work?" She offered this partly to be nice, but more to be able to keep track of what Chase was doing and keep him focused on what she needed.

"Sure, that'd be great. I'll see you then," Chase said and he hung up.

Chase spent most of the rest of the afternoon searching the web for any indication of an impending bomb threat in the L.A. area. He didn't find anything. Eventually, for lack of any other leads, he searched for evidence of Pinkies. That search wasn't very successful, either. He found the usual rumors about the Pinkies that kept the urban legend alive. Besides that, all he found was an obscure reference to the Pinkies in a Wikipedia article about the Secret Service. But that only said that there was no such thing as Pinkies. He found the need to say that there was no such thing as Pinkies in a Secret Service article a little unnecessary.

Chapter 11
(The Recent Past)

Fidele Veritas felt a wave of dizziness. *That could be from nerves*, he thought to himself. After all, he was arming a nuclear bomb. But he had been preparing for this for a long time – his whole life, in a way, in that he had recently realized that all his life events had been pointing him toward this moment. So, it probably wasn't nerves so much. He was also worried that he had gotten a deep radiation dose when he was working with the device a few days ago. He had been very careful, as usual, and his Geiger counter hadn't indicated any excessive radiation. But he was working in pretty cramped quarters and his Geiger counter was old. So, he wasn't completely sure he had been careful enough. In any case, it didn't matter. He could fight through the dizziness and finish his job.

He knew that he *must* finish his job. He knew that if he didn't, he would be failing his one and only true God. It was his commitment to his one and only true God that made him choose the name Fidele Veritas. He thought of naming himself something like Sergei Romanoff as a nod toward the soviets during the Cold War, or something like Muhammad El Sader as a nod toward America's more recent nemesis, the terrorists of the Middle East. One of those names would have helped start the finger pointing after the bomb went off. But he finally settled on Fidele Veritas because of a passage from the Revelation of Saint John the Divine, the final book of the Christian Bible: "Then I saw heaven opened, and there was a white horse! Its rider is called Faithful and True, and in righteousness he judges and makes war. His eyes are like a flame of fire, and on his head are many diadems; and he has a name inscribed that no one knows but himself." Fidele means 'Faithful' and Veritas means 'Truth'.

The name didn't matter, anyway, because the only people who knew it were the few men who smuggled the bomb out of a nuclear weapons maintenance facility in Russia during a vulnerable point in the chaos following the fall of the Soviet Union and eventually sold it to Fidele Veritas. And they were all dead now due to a series of unfortunate accidents. Fidele Veritas knew the finger pointing would start anyway.

Fidele Veritas had trained himself not to feel any emotion when it came to this mission. He knew that if he felt any emotion at all, he would feel intense guilt because of the millions of innocent people he was about to kill. But if he had let himself feel intense guilt, he still could have reasoned that he had tried peaceful ways to get people to realize that their apathetic, selfish, plain old unconcerned lives were fucking the world up so much that if they didn't knock it off, there would be no turning back. If they didn't knock it off, the whole earth would eventually end up as a barren wasteland like Los Angeles after his bomb went off. So, in a way, what he was doing was their fault.

His choice of Los Angeles showed that, even though he wouldn't let himself feel any emotion at all when it came to this mission, he still let himself be patriotic. He still wanted the good old U.S. of A. to emerge victorious from the World War III that he would soon start. So, he couldn't take out a city like Washington DC, the political capital of the good old U.S. of A., or like New York, the financial capital. So, he made the next best choice, Los Angeles, the entertainment capital. That would be adequate to fulfill his God-given mission, he thought.

Another wave of dizziness washed over Fidele Veritas, this one noticeably worse than the first, this time with nausea added in. *Shit, I must have seriously dosed myself,* he thought to himself. *Luckily, this will only take another minute, or so.* He sat up straighter in the back of his Humvee, trying to beat the dizziness, and keyed in his access code. This was the same Humvee he had stored his bomb in for the past several weeks. What better place to 'hide' a car like this than the student parking garage of an affluent university, where cars sit for weeks on end anyway.

A third wave of nauseous dizziness overcame Fidele Veritas. His eyes were watering now. It was all he could do to set the date he wanted into the timer he had added a few days ago and press the red button to start the timer ticking, completing the arming sequence. He had meant to enter a date three days in the future to give him time to attend to some final business and leave the city. But, because he was now fighting desperately to just stay conscious, he wasn't completely sure what date he had set and there was nothing he could do about it. He stumbled out of his Humvee for a final time, staggered home, and fell forward on his living room floor. Just as he was losing consciousness, he thought, *I did it, God*!

And the timer ticked on...

Chapter 12
(The Present)

Lacey arrived at Chase's a little after 8:00 PM with Double-Doubles, fries, and strawberry shakes in hand, just as she had promised.

"Excellent, strawberry, my favorite," said Chase.

Lacey didn't bother saying, "*I know.*" She figured she'd freaked him out enough demonstrating how thorough her investigation of him had been, including mild stalking, after her father spoke his name. Instead she said, "So, have you found anything out?"

"Gee, you don't waste any time, do you?" Chase said. "Come on in so we can eat, at least." Chase led Lacey to a large chocolate-brown couch that dominated the living room of the house he shared with two other UCLA students and that was, of course, pointed directly at a large flat screen TV with a PlayStation and an Xbox connected to it. The living room itself was plain, with beige carpets and off-white walls. There was a couple of surfing posters haphazardly put up on the walls. But, otherwise, the walls were bare. There was a small square table at one end of the couch. On the other side of that end-table was an old wood and leather armchair that was actually more comfortable than it looked and that was also, of course, pointed toward the TV. Besides a tuna can and a soda can on the end-table, it, along with the rest of the room, was pretty neat considering it was heavily used by three college students. There was a coffee table in front of the couch that also served as a dinner table as often as not, including tonight.

Chase was about one bite into his burger when Lacy asked again, "Okay, so have you found anything out?"

"Not really," Chase answered. He somewhat hesitantly told her about the obscure reference to Pinkies that he had found.

"Aha!" she said, "So you're starting to believe me!"

"No, not really," Chase answered. He expected that reaction from her and that's why he had been somewhat hesitant to tell her. "But I wanted to try to follow all leads. I'll try to dig deeper tomorrow."

"Tomorrow? What's wrong with tonight?"

"Lacey," Chase answered, "I like you and I'm starting to want to help you. But I do have school and stuff. I have homework to do."

"Oh, right, homework and stuff," Lacey said gloomily. "I guess I shouldn't keep you, then." She started to get up, putting her mostly uneaten food back in the bag.

"No, that's okay," Chase said quickly. "I don't have to do it this second. Stick around for a little while. There's a question I've been wanting to ask you anyway. Yesterday, you said your father was getting into some pretty deep stuff. What did you mean by that?"

"Oh, that," Lacey said. "Yeah, a few years ago he got the idea that he could fix the world and he actually started trying to do it. You know how people say, 'this is wrong' or 'that's wrong' and 'somebody should really do something about it'? Well, my father decided he was the *somebody*. The crazy thing is that people started buying into it. He started organizing rallies on campus and people started coming – eventually a lot of people. His little crusade started spreading way beyond the campus, too."

"All kinds of people fight for all kinds of causes, Lacey," Chase said. "What made your father's cause deep?"

"There are several dimensions to my father's thinking. But what he's been making the most noise about is that, in his opinion, *our political and economic systems are fundamentally flawed.* Believe me, these are strong words coming from a through-and-through American. My dad's a decorated veteran for Christ's sake."

"What does *fundamentally flawed* mean?" Chase asked.

"In a word," Lacey answered, "it means that our systems are selfish. They let the people with the big money and the power – which for my dad are the same thing – manipulate the system to best suit *them*."

"That's not all big-money's fault, you know. If everyone was more active and involved, it would be harder for the big-money to do whatever it wanted. But –"

Lacey interrupted Chase as her stomach sank a little bit, "Wait, you said you never knew my dad, right?"

"Yeah, I told you," Chase said with a touch of annoyance in his voice. "I know about him from the news and some of my friends have had him for classes. Otherwise, I didn't know him. Why do you ask again?"

"My father would have said the exact same thing. I was just wondering if he had talked to you about it."

"No, we never talked," Chase said. "But I wasn't done yet. I was going to also say that big-money takes advantage of most people's apathy. If they can keep most people just comfortable enough that they continue not to give much of a crap, then they can do pretty much whatever they want to. It's a continual balancing act."

Luckily for Lacey's stomach there was stuff in the way, or it probably would have sunk into the floor by now. Unfortunately for her head, a lot of the blood that was usually up there went down to help hold her stomach up – she was feeling a bit faint. What Chase was saying was very close to what her father said. Lacey was very rarely wrong, but could she have misunderstood her father's intentions for Chase? Was he supposed to continue her father's crusade rather than chase after bombs and Pinkies? She would need to probe his ideas further. But first she needed to figure out if there was a possible intellectual link between her father and him. "Do you talk to people about politics and stuff?" she asked.

"Yeah, I talk to people about this stuff. I usually talk about it in a hypothetical sense, though. Even in America, it's not too smart to say too loudly that your government is fundamentally flawed," Chase answered.

Yeah, I think my father's finding that out, Lacey thought. "Another thing my father says," she continued, "is that humanity is still warlike, like it's been since man first realized he was erect. The only difference is that today's battles are mostly waged in back rooms and board rooms, rather than on battle fields. But the people still suffer when the commanders fuck up and the commanders seem to fuck up pretty often. Is that what you think, too?"

"That's how your father says it?" asked Chase.

"I may have paraphrased a little," Lacey answered.

"Well, I wouldn't put it exactly that way. But, yeah, that's pretty much right," Chase said. "Are you okay?"

"No, I'm not so great right now," Lacey said. "I have to go. See you tomorrow, maybe." Lacey headed for the door.

"Yeah, okay, see you," Chase said. "Thanks for the food..." he added. But Lacey was gone.

And the timer ticked on...

Chapter 13
(The Future)

"Wait," Kurt ordered. "I need to net Jennifer."

"No problem, go right ahead," said Kurt's father, remembering why he loved having his son around, but also didn't mind too much when he left.

Kurt turned his attention inward to neuro-net his child-mate, the woman he would be having a baby with soon, or so they hoped. When he returned his attention to his father there was a pained look on his face that he couldn't completely hide.

"What's wrong?" his father asked.

"If you really must know," Kurt responded with a combination of anger and annoyance in his voice, "I'm getting knocked down another level."

"Knocked down another level?" Kurt's father said, incensed, his fatherly pride trumping his son's nearly continual ill-temper. "But your work is first rate! It always has been. How can they possibly justify knocking you down? You were pretty high for your age, weren't you?"

"Yeah, I was doing okay," Kurt responded. "I was at 17 a couple of years ago."

Since many people are likely to be reading this in the Present, rather than the Future, a few words of explanation are probably in order. Soon after the Catalyst event (more on this later), many things began to change. One thing that changed was that nearly everyone explicitly acknowledged that all people are entitled to enough of the earth's resources to survive, with at least some small amount of comfort. And, further, that no person should need to depend on the whim and wisdom, or lack thereof, of the rulers of the day to receive those resources. In other words, people should not need to live in continual fear of losing their paychecks, and not being able to put food on their tables, because of the current rulers' latest economic screw-up or because another country has been found to exploit for cheap labor.

The level at which people receive enough of the earth's resources to survive, with at least some small amount of comfort, is level zero. Level zero used to be called the Subsistence level. But, because of the negative connotations of that word, it's now called the Existence level. There are 24 levels above Existence that people achieve by their contributions to the arts, sciences, or business. A person's level determines how nice a house they can live in and how many credits they get a week for food, fun, etc.

There are a couple of costs that go along with a guaranteed share of the earth's resources (or at least what people considered costs before they got used to them). The first cost is that, if you're not otherwise employed and there's something that absolutely needs to be done and there's absolutely no one else on earth to do it and you have the ability to do it, you can be recruited to do it and there's really nothing you can say about it. The only choice you have is whether you want to do the work in freedom or prison. Most things that need to be done these days get done. So recruiting is rarely necessary. When it is, people usually choose freedom rather than prison. The second cost is that it now takes more than a happy ending on the slip and slide ride to make a baby, even if making a baby is what a couple is trying to do.

"So what level are you now?" Kurt's father asked.

"Well, now I'm a 14, I guess," Kurt answered.

"Down 3 levels in two years. That's absurd! What happened?"

"They say they moved me up too fast based on my graduate work. They say they overestimated my 'genius'."

"Oh, that's ridiculous. Your work was groundbreaking. People have been trying to resolve the Tubingen Inconsistency for twenty years and you did it in two."

Chapter 14
(The Future)

Actually, Kurt's father was being generous. Kurt had made progress toward resolving the Tubingen Inconsistency. But he hadn't conclusively resolved it. The Tubingen Inconsistency was the latest manifestation of the decades-old question: Do machines that aren't made of flesh and bones and blood have a soul or not? The inconsistency was that some recent experiments had gone one way and others had gone the other. It was named after Tubingen University, where a conference had been held to address the issue several years ago. Not completely by coincidence, Tubingen also housed the equipment that Kurt used for his research.

The English name for the equipment that Kurt used was the Complete Human Brain Simulator, or CHuBS for short, along with the Complete Human Body Replica, or CHuBR. CHuBS was a room full of computer hardware that had processing power, memory, and interconnects equivalent to a human brain and was designed to functionally match. CHuBS had artificial eyes that connected to image processing hardware occupying a percentage of its artificial brain equivalent to the percentage of a human brain used for the same purpose, artificial ears with a matching percentage of artificial brain, artificial arms, etc. The artificial eyes, ears, arms, etc. were physically part of CHuBR, a respectable, although still clearly artificial, robotic imitation of a human body. CHuBS and CHuBR were connected by several high-speed RF satellite links. The CHuBS / CHuBR combination had been affectionately nicknamed Chubby some years back, partly because of its official names and partly because of its big fat brain.

Chubby was getting on in age by the time Kurt used it, which, frankly, is why he could use it at all. Several similar systems had been built at other research institutions, each smaller than the last, with the promise of a self-contained unit in only a few more years. Most established researchers were using the newer systems. Realizing this, Tubingen put out a call for graduate research proposals for work on Chubby about five years ago. Kurt, who had completed his undergraduate degree in Computer Science at MIT in record time and at the top of his class, applied and was given two years of exclusive use of Chubby, an unprecedented amount even given Chubby's advanced age.

What Kurt proposed to do (and did) was to spend most of the years "bringing up" Chubby as if from a baby. Most of what Chubby had been used for prior to Kurt was to perform nature versus nurture experiments. This was done by pre-programming Chubby with various initial conditions ranging from virtually none to virtually fully-formed and then subjecting it to carefully orchestrated experiences. Using this research, Kurt produced a pre-program that put Chubby in a state that perfectly emulated a newborn infant and then 'birthed' him ('him', because Kurt flipped an old penny his father had given him when he was young and Chubby became a boy – Kurt was glad fate made Chubby a boy because, even in his day of complete gender equality, he still felt better referring to a male as 'Chubby' than a female).

Kurt spent the better part of the next two years teaching Chubby and interacting with him, developing him to early adulthood. Even Kurt's largest detractors, and he had several as his project progressed, agreed that Chubby perfectly emulated a human being, even though his development had been greatly accelerated. Chubby had wants and needs, he laughed and cried, he had intelligence, he had creativity, he had dreams both literally and figuratively; he appeared to be perfectly human.

Then, Kurt ran a psychological experiment. He recruited twenty subjects, one of whom was Chubby. He asked the twenty subjects to sit down, close their eyes, and clear their minds of all earthly thoughts and concerns. He then asked the subjects to look deep down into themselves to see whether there was anything there; possibly an essence, an 'I', a sense of self. Nineteen of the twenty subjects answered that yes, there was an essence, an 'I', a sense of self. The one who answered no was Chubby.

Kurt concluded that he had demonstrated that a machine that was not flesh and bone and blood, but was human in every other way, did not have the spark of life, a spirit, a soul and, therefore, had shown that only flesh and bone and blood humans have souls. There was controversy around this, of course. Although their numbers were greatly diminished, there were still some who thought that even flesh and bone and blood humans don't have souls and, therefore, Kurt proved nothing. There were others who claimed that Kurt's pre-program simply lacked the few lines of code needed to let Chubby realize that he had a soul. Even Kurt realized that a single demonstration does not constitute a proof and, so, didn't claim that he 'proved' his thesis. But he and most others believed that his was a very important result.

Chapter 15
(The Future)

"Yeah, I know my graduate work was groundbreaking and I know my current work is first rate," Kurt said. "My being knocked down has nothing to do with my work. I'm being knocked down as punishment for being a radical Indie and doing something about it."

Indies were people concerned more about individual rights than society, even if those rights let some people live wildly affluent lives while others live on the streets. Socios were people concerned more about society. 'Socio' started as a derogatory term, suggesting, ironically, that Socios were sociopaths with no concern for the consequences of their actions. But the name stuck. Being an Indie was considered being selfish and inconsistent with humanity's increased post-Catalyst maturity. There weren't too many Indies left in Kurt's day, but there were some and he was one of them. Kurt was, in fact, a strong Indie and very vocal about it. Vocal enough that he'd been attracting quite a following.

"Son, I find that very hard to believe. You know as well as I do that there are many safeguards to assure that the granting of levels isn't abused. The Board of Governors has nothing to gain or lose. They're all at level 18 for life. Not to mention that they are all people of the highest integrity. Even if they weren't, there are strict rules for advancing and downgrading people. If all that fails, of course, there are peer reviews. Have you requested a review?"

"My request from the last time I was downgraded was denied because I was still above the average for a Computer Scientist two years out of graduate school. Since I'm still in the range of where I should be, I probably won't waste my time again. No matter how you slice it, Dad, everybody knows there's some subjectivity in assigning levels and that's hard to fight. Maybe I just plain old pissed someone off and now I'm paying for it."

Kurt's father wanted to say, "*You, piss someone off? You think? Maybe?*" But, instead, he said, "Well, be that as it may, dropping 3 levels in two years is unheard of. That should help you out some, if you want to appeal again. Are you going to have to move?"

"Probably," answered Kurt. "Last time, Jennifer was going up as I was going down, which saved us. That won't happen this time. So, I expect we'll need to move to a lower level house." Kurt's face started to get red as the anger that had subsided while he and his father talked came back. He continued heatedly, "Do you see why I hate this system? In the old days, if I worked hard, I would have been successful. And if I were successful, I would have bought a house. And if I bought a house, it would have been mine. And if it was mine, no one could have taken it away from me, God damn it!"

"That's not necessarily true. Your *if*s need to be prefaced by a very big one: In the old days, if you were in the right geographical, political, and financial place and time, then what you said may have been true. But being in the right place and time was pretty random and it was the exception rather than the rule.

"By the way, although I'll admit that I can't see any other reason, I still can't accept that your being downgraded is political punishment. That kind of thing is ancient history now. But, if it were true, I guess there wouldn't be any sense in pointing out that if you weren't fighting the system this wouldn't be happening."

"You're right, Dad. There wouldn't be any sense in pointing that out."

"Well, at least you're still way above Existence," said Kurt's father, trying to look at his son's glass as 60% full rather than 40% empty. Trying to lighten the mood, he said, "By the way, I do have a bit of good news. Uncle Greg and Aunt Gail got approved for a third the other day." Greg and Gail weren't actually Kurt's aunt and uncle, his father didn't have any siblings, but they were close friends.

"Dad, do you know me at all? Do you think it's really good news to me that Greg and Gail need to be *approved* to have a damned baby? I can't stand that the government intrudes in people's lives so much!

That's exactly the kind of thing I've been fighting. Anyway, go on with your story... please!"

"Part of the reason I told you is they'll be stopping by later. Just to let you know..."

Chapter 16
(The Present)

The day after she abruptly left Chase's house, Lacey was conflicted about whether to go see him or not. She wasn't sure what her father had in mind for him, whether it was to search for bombs and Pinkies or to carry on his crusade for the common person, or maybe both. But she had to find out. So late in the afternoon she went over to his house.

Chase smiled when he opened the door. "Hi," he said. "I wasn't sure I was going to see you. You tore out of here pretty quickly last night."

"Yeah, I wasn't feeling so great. I need to ask you some questions. Can I come in?"

"Sure, of course," Chase answered. They went into the living room and sat down. "I'm glad you're here because I have some really interesting things to tell you," Chase said, trying hard to mask his excitement.

"Okay, but let me go first." Lacey had a set of questions lined up in her head. "Do you think it's right that some people make millions or even billions of dollars, while other people make barely enough to scrape by, or less?"

"To answer that, you need to think about what money's really for. Is money to reward people for being in the right place at the right time and also to perpetuate dynasties? Or is money to be traded for people's productive work so that they can, in turn, exchange it for the necessities and pleasures of life and also to support people who, for whatever reason, can't do productive work?"

"What do you mean by 'being in the right place at the right time'?" Lacey asked.

"As the standard example, let's consider Jill Bates, the gal who made her billions with Screens, the computer operating system everybody loves to hate. Jill didn't start out with much and is now worth a few billion dollars. So, in one way or another, Jill was compensated with at least that much. Let's be generous and say that the average person is compensated with a few million dollars in his or her lifetime. That's around a thousand times difference. So, does that mean that Jill is a thousand times smarter than the average person, or a thousand times more capable, or works a thousand times harder, or works a thousand times more hours a week, or some combination of those? No, of course not, that's absurd. What it means is that Jill was in just the right time: the dawn of the personal computer revolution. And it means that Jill was in just the right place: in the country where the personal computer revolution started and in close enough proximity to another less marketing-savvy software company from which she could license

Screens' predecessor operating system for little more than a song.

"Similar things can be said about corporate executives and financial people. They're in a relatively prosperous time and in a place where, for whatever reason, society permits them to pay themselves absurd amounts of money and/or find the latest barely-legal, mostly-immoral ways to beat the system to their own considerable benefit: junk bonds, accounting shell games, and subprime mortgages being just a few examples.

"A usually less sinister version of this theme describes the often mediocre people who come by large sums of money by simply being born into it rather than by any positive attributes or contributions of their own. That's what I mean by 'being in the right place at the right time' and 'perpetuating dynasties'. So, hopefully, you're getting the answer to your question. I don't think it's right that some people make dump trucks full of money while other people live on the streets.

"At the very least, maybe the amount paid to the highest earners in a company, including all forms of compensation, should be limited to 100 times the amount paid to the lowest. That means that if the lowest paid people made 10 dollars an hour, a barely livable wage anywhere, the highest paid people would be limited to the equivalent of 1,000 dollars an hour, or about two million dollars a year. The clever executive, by the way, would realize that an easy way to give him or herself a raise would be to pay the lowest on the totem pole a more livable wage."

"Sure," said Lacey, "and then executives start spinning off separate management companies that simply manage their original companies, or take their businesses to other countries."

"Yes, yes, as I alluded to before, there are always barely-legal, mostly-immoral ways to beat the system. Maybe our top business schools should spend more time drilling ethics into students than the ultra-competitive arrogance that translates into *must win at any cost* selfishness. Maybe the first five words they teach in business school should be the first five words they teach in medical school: ABOVE ALL, DO NO HARM. As far as executives taking their businesses to other countries is concerned, in the short term let them go – as long as the executives go with their businesses. The reasons people prefer living in the United States transcend its business-friendliness. In the longer term, it's time to start dismantling the arbitrary borders that made some sense when the world was big, but make less and less sense as the world gets smaller and smaller."

Lacey said, "Although your reasoning is different than my father's, you get to pretty much the same answer."

"Is that what this is all about?" asked Chase.

"Yeah, pretty much."

Chapter 17
(The Present)

"Okay," Lacey said, "my next question is, what do you think about our consumer driven economy?"

"Wait, do you want something to drink or anything?" Chase asked. "I'm getting kind of thirsty."

"No, I'm good. I really kind of want to get through this. So, what do you think about our consumer driven economy?"

"Okay, fine, I'll suffer. To answer your question, I think that, since our earth has limited natural resources, an economic system that is only healthy if its people consume resources as fast as they possibly can isn't sustainable. About the only way it could be sustainable would be if absolutely everything were recycled and energy were completely renewable. And that doesn't seem feasible at this point in time. To make matters worse, because the economy depends on consumption, if people don't consume as fast as they can, they lose their jobs, they lose their homes, they lose their food, and they lose whatever security they once had. That seems kind of stupid to me. We have to find a better way!"

"Yeah, you work on that. So, what do people do if they're not busy making the stuff for people to use and for rich people to make profits on?"

"I don't know. Stop and smell the roses, I guess," Chase answered.

"I mean for work, wise ass."

"I still don't know. Maybe there just isn't enough work now for most people to spend forty hours a week or more doing it. Maybe the way work is apportioned and the way people are compensated need to be re-thought. When you think about it, with the exception of some labor laws and the like, the way we're doing things now dates back to the Industrial Revolution. Maybe things need to be revised for the Technical Revolution or, beyond that, the Environmental Revolution."

"Do you think this would all be better if people were more proactive for the common good?"

"Oh, definitely. Lots of people tend to be pretty lethargic when it comes to societal matters. A lot of the time people can't really be blamed for that, though. After spending long days working, people often have the energy to have a beer and a quick dinner, kiss the kids, and go to bed to get ready for the next day on the hamster wheel and that's about it. Again, we have to find a better way!" Chase was starting to like that statement.

"That's the second or third time you've said something like 'chasing the almighty buck is what everybody spends their lives doing.' That's pretty sad. Don't you think there's anything more to life?"

"I'm saying that people should *not* have to spend their lives chasing the almighty buck. But that's what people end up *doing*. And, yes, it is sad! That's the damn point!

"Think about what money is for a minute. What is money? A small amount of money is *survival*: like you have food, clothes, and shelter. A medium amount of money is *security*: like you don't need to live from paycheck to paycheck and you have enough for retirement. A large amount of money is *power*: like you say what everybody's operating system will do and won't do and you have a big say about who your next Senator will be.

"The lower class worries most about the first of these and a little about the middle. The middle class worries most about the middle of these and a little about the first and last. The upper class worries most about the last of these and a little about the middle. But the point is, everybody worries about money. It shouldn't have to be like that!"

"Yeah, yeah, I know," said Lacey, "we have to find a better way! Although you get to things in different ways, what you get to is hauntingly similar to what my father says." At this point, she was pretty sure her father had chosen Chase to carry on his crusade and that's why he said his name.

Chapter 18
(The Present)

"Okay, so is it my turn now?" asked Chase.

"No, I have one more question. What is God?"

"What is God? Are you sure that's your last question? Are you sure you don't want to ask what the meaning of life is after that?"

"Yeah, maybe we'll get to that one," said Lacey. "It depends on how you do with this one."

"God," Chase started, "is two facets of a diamond: the punishing, tough love facet of the Old Testament and the forgiving, love your neighbor facet of the New Testament. Both of those facets are brilliant and beautiful. But they are nothing compared to the brilliance and beauty of the whole diamond, if people would just look at it. The whole diamond undulates, it pulsates, it moves, it flows, if people would just let it. I and others like to call this diamond the spirit. The spirit is permeating, ingrained, overarching – humanity needs to be in synchronicity with it. But we're not.

"Most religions that claim to worship God, or Allah, or Vishnu, or Whoever do the spirit a disservice because they concretize it. Christians, for example, place so much emphasis on the flowing of the spirit through Jesus (as it undoubtedly did – mightily) they don't spend much time realizing that it can flow mightily through them, too. The spirit can flow through any and all of us, but, admittedly, it takes work. In particular, it takes faith, prayer, and action. The most striking –"

"Wait, wait," said Lacey, "'faith', isn't that a perilous word for a scientist?"

"What do you mean?"

"I mean, you consider yourself a scientist, right?"

"Yeah, I do."

"And don't scientists accept only what they can see and hear and smell and taste and touch?"

"I guess some scientists think they do."

"What do you mean?"

"People go beyond what their senses tell them every second of every day. For example, people have to have faith that things in the future will happen as they have in the past with nothing to base that on except that that's just how it's always been. Like, what do you prove when you throw a ball in the air and it falls back down?"

"Well, the law of gravity, of course, Isaac," Lacey said referring to Isaac Newton of falling apple fame.

"Wrong! You demonstrate gravity, but you don't prove anything. You can throw a ball up in the air and have it fall back down a million times and all you'll get out of it is a severely sore arm, because there's absolutely no guarantee that on the millionth-and-first throw that ball won't just keep going straight up. You have to have faith that it won't!"

"Yeah, I know."

"What do you mean you know?"

"I mean, I know. I know you can't prove something by demonstrating it a zillion times. I was just testing you."

"Did I pass?" asked Chase.

"Yeah, you passed."

"Okay," Chase said, "so you agree that, without something as farfetched as time travel, there's no way to even demonstrate that the physical laws of the future will be the same as the laws of the past, right? So, it needs to be taken on faith, right? Is it such a stretch to take God on faith just because you can't physically see or hear or smell or taste or touch God?"

"Wait, why do you say time travel is farfetched? That's something I can actually believe in."

"Oh, brother," Chase said, not really wanting to get sucked into the time travel debate. "There are so many problems with time travel, it's barely worth discussing. Like, think about it, let's say time travel became possible. Wouldn't people from every generation thereafter want to witness historic events? Like, wouldn't people want to witness the birth or death of religious figures, like Moses or Jesus or Muhammad, or watch the launch of Apollo 11, or be there for the landing of the lunar module, Eagle, for that matter, or witness the ends of the World Wars? Wouldn't those events and countless others be ridiculously crowded with future-people?"

"Well, no," Lacey answered, "because there would be strict controls put in place."

Chase chuckled and said, "Strict controls? Have you ever met the human race? Strict controls are violated all the time." Chase didn't wait for a response. "And what about the *future people changing their own past* argument? That argument goes way beyond the macro examples given on TV shows, by the way. For example, what if a time traveler accidentally moved a pebble and that pebble caused a man to slip just the slightest bit and that caused the man to make love to his wife two seconds later than he would have if he hadn't slipped and that, in turn, caused another sperm to win the race for life? A completely different child would be born to that man and woman just because a time traveler accidentally moved a pebble. The seemingly most trivial events could and would have profound consequences. In fact, I don't think a time traveler could *ever* go back in time and *not* change the future."

"You make valid points," Lacey said. "But, I still can't rule out the possibility of time travel. I'm sorry."

Chase breathed out hard, trying to control his agitation. He took a couple of breaths, but it didn't help much. "You can believe in the possibility of time travel, with considerable arguments against it, but not the possibility of God? You're a prime example of our severely science-centric society. Science has lifted the veil from a minute portion of our physical universe, including our world, and all of a sudden it's the be all and end all of everything. Now, don't get me wrong, Lacey, I'm as big a fan of science as anyone. I just can't let it rule out the possibility of things it can't explain, at least yet."

"Are you finished?" Lacey asked. "I'm not saying I'm not enjoying seeing your face get all red and the veins pop out of your neck. I pretty much am. I'm just checking whether you're finished."

"Yeah, I guess I am," Chase said, feeling himself calming down. "Sorry to get all bent out of shape. The whole God/science dichotomy just frustrates me sometimes. So, anyway, setting all this philosophical mumbo-jumbo aside, do you have faith? I mean do you have faith in the *faith, prayer, and action* sense?"

"Well, it's nice of you to ask, since you've already condemned me for my beliefs without really knowing what they are."

"You're right. I did do that," responded Chase. "I just got an idea of what you believe from the way you were talking. So, I apologize. So, what do you believe?"

"I don't know, really. If I can say so without getting my science-centric head chopped off, I've never really felt a need for the whole 'God' thing. God might have been a comfort when my mother was killed. But even then, I didn't feel the need."

"So, you feel there's nothing deeper in life than the here-we-are-on-earth physical part?"

"I don't really know."

"Okay, you need to do something for me," said Chase.

"Forget it, buddy, I barely even know you."

"Very funny. But I'm serious. Shut your eyes and relax. Just sit there for a while and try to clear your mind." Lacey sat for several minutes in as close to a meditative state as she could achieve. "Is your mind clear?" Lacey nodded slightly. "Now with your mind still clear, sink as deeply into yourself as you can. ... Are you there?" Lacey nodded again. "Is there anything there? Are *you* there? Can you sense your *self*?"

"Yeah, kind of," Lacey answered faintly.

"Okay, you can open your eyes. So, do you think that your *self*, your *essence* can be explained by neurons, neurotransmitters, and electric impulses?"

Lacey opened her eyes and shook her head as if to shake cobwebs out. "Okay, I'll admit it, there might be a bit more to me than can be explained by flesh, blood, brain cells, and synapses. But I'm still not very convinced."

"Okay, well you can't blame a guy for trying. So, can I get back to what I was saying before I was so rudely interrupted?" Chase asked.

"Yeah, I *guess* so," Lacey answered with teasing sarcasm.

"The most striking example of the concretization of the spirit, literally, is the church. As with most bu-reaucracies, the church became more concerned with its own preservation than with its original purpose. A specific case in point is that churches become more concerned with their buildings than their missions. As a church dies, it's almost always its building that's last to go, not its feeding the hungry or housing the homeless. To my recollection, Jesus did not say, 'Go out and maintain nice buildings.' The spirit flowed through the church most effectively in its early days, when people met in homes, before the political and religious aristocracies got their gilded hands on it and bent it to their own purposes.

"Another less literal concretization of the spirit comes when ancient books are put on inappropriately high pedestals. These books, like the Christian Bible, for example, document powerful interactions between people and the spirit and offer valuable guidance for life. But to think that they represent the beginning, middle, and end of humanity's interactions with the spirit and that they are the exclusive and authoritative Word of God is absurd and often impedes the free flowing of the spirit in the present.

"I guess giving the Bible and like books such authority is convenient for people who want things wrapped up in nice tidy little packages. But life just isn't like that. It's also helpful for those who feel a need to stand between the spirit and the 'common man' by claiming a superior ability to interpret and apply the books, like the priests of the past and the present. But nobody should stand between anyone and the spirit.

Everyone should have a direct, active, and intimate relationship with the spirit.

"Giving the Bible and like books too much authority runs other risks, too. Like messages that made sense when they were given can be carried into times when they no longer make sense and can even become destructive. Like, 'be fruitful and multiply' made perfect sense when humanity was young and struggling to establish its foothold in a savage world. But now that humanity is being fruitful and multiplying itself to death, it doesn't make sense any more. Still, some prominent religions forbid their followers from using the spirit's gift of birth control partly because of that ancient statement. It's truly insane."

"Well, at least this is one place where your thoughts differ from my father's," Lacey said. "Your thinking is way more sophisticated than his. He has this kind of conventional love hate relationship with God and Jesus. Sometimes he seems to be a flaming atheist, like, even if there is a god, that god has so forsaken him at some time in his life that there's no sense in believing. Sometimes he seems to be a completely devoted Christian, trying desperately to atone for something terrible he's done in his life, maybe in Vietnam. Sometimes he seems to be both. I never have quite figured it out. I think the second of these is why he's felt compelled to start his little crusade, though.

"So, you had something to tell me?"

Chapter 19
(The Present)

Chase said, "I found it kind of strange that there was a statement in a Secret Service article denying that there were Pinkies. So, this morning I poked around a little bit. I found my way into the classified Secret Service LAN and then I found my way into the inner sanctum of the Pinky program. There is a lot of stuff in there!"

"You *found your way* into the classified Secret Service LAN? How did you do that?"

"Well, I'd tell you," Chase said with a bit of pride forcing its way into his smile, "but then I'd have to shoot you."

"Oh, come on, you don't have to give me all your dirty little secrets. Just give me a hint."

"To make a long story short, I found an old Unix server with an unprotected backdoor, still on the public side of the Secret Service firewall. That was the easy part. The hard part was finding a vulnerable server in the Pinky inner sanctum and hacking into it. Once I did that, though, it was relatively easy to navigate around. I found a ton of information. What I've found so far are scans of old records going back nearly fifty years. I've found the code names for the Pinky agents, although not a whole lot more about them, yet. There seem to have been five Pinkies, not two, by the way. Although, only three still seem to be active. There's even information about current assignments."

"So, you waited until now to tell me this?" Lacey said with excitement and more than a tinge of irritation in her voice.

Chase gave her a, "*You've gotta be kidding me!*" look, but otherwise didn't say anything.

"Okay, you're right... sorry," she said. "So, log onto the site. Come on, let's explore!"

"We really shouldn't do that. If I use my way in sparingly and carefully, I should be able to stay undetected. If you or I start poking around a lot, someone's bound to notice and, at best, they'll shut down my access. At worst, they'll figure out it's me hacking in and then I'm sunk."

"Okay, I'm sure you're right'" said Lacey. "So, was there anything about a bomb or anything?"

"No, nothing about a bomb."

"That's too bad," said Lacey. "Well, it's getting late and I'm pretty tired. I should be getting home."

"You can stay here, if you want," said Chase.

"Thanks, stud, but I should go home."

Chase's face got a little red, partly because what Lacey thought wasn't what he meant at all. But also because if he had thought about it for even a millisecond, that's exactly what he would have meant. He was a little flustered, "No, wait, I mean, um, I just thought you might not want to stay in your house all alone."

"How do you know I'd be all alone?"

Chase thought about it for a second and wasn't sure. "I don't know," he said. "I just thought you were an only child. You haven't mentioned any brothers or sisters. Do you have any?"

"No, I don't," answered Lacey.

"So, you'd be staying in your house all alone?"

"Yes."

"Then, what the heck are you jerking me around for?"

"I don't know. I just don't like when people assume," said Lacey. "Anyway, I'll see you later."

"Yeah, okay, later," Chase said, half glad Lacey wasn't staying over. Well, probably not half, maybe a quarter. Well, probably not even a quarter. Actually, he wished she was staying.

And the timer ticked on...

Chapter 20
(The Future)

"Dad," Kurt said, "I have to take a break. I have to go to the bathroom." He stood up to go. "Sorry," he added as an afterthought.

While Kurt was in the bathroom, his father considered Kurt's situation. Nearly everyone on the planet realized that the ways of the past were destructive to people and the earth and that present-day ways were much better. But Kurt was an exception and his father couldn't figure out why. He had been raised well, if his father did say so himself. He had gone to good schools – although he had, admittedly, gotten through them faster than most. Maybe that wasn't such a good idea. He hadn't been denied anything substantial that his father could think of. But he always had a fiercely individualistic streak, to the point of rebelliousness. There's a theory that, as every person develops, he or she passes through every stage of evolutionary development from a single celled organism to a mature human adult. It's as though Kurt got stuck in the decades old stage characterized by fierce individualism.

Most people had advanced to a maturity that included enough faith in the future so as not to spend most of their lives clawing for every possible shred of materialistic security and, along with that, enough selflessness to put individualism aside. This wasn't the fanatic, impractical *give everything to the poor and follow me* selflessness of the past, but rather a more balanced *I care as much about you as I care about me* selflessness. Kurt's father was sad to think that Kurt couldn't be counted among *most people*. To make matters worse, Kurt was preaching his individualism and gaining some converts, including his child-mate, Jennifer. Although, maybe going along with him was the only way Jennifer could stand him. Wait, that wasn't nice. Kurt's father took that last thought back.

Kurt's independence made it hard for him to accept many aspects of the new world order. For example, it was hard for him to accept that he couldn't own anything – actually, nobody could. It's not that the government owned everything and doled things out as it saw fit. It's that nobody owned anything. People used things as they needed them, like the Native Americans had used the gifts of the land, water, and air when they needed them (when there was such a thing as Native Americans). One thing that this meant, that particularly irked Kurt, was that people couldn't leave their possessions to their children anymore. Now, when someone passes on, what he or she had been using reverts to the pool of available stuff for other worthy people to use. Kurt's father had tried explaining over and over that this makes more sense because it means that the materialistic quality of a person's life depends on his or her abilities and how he or she chooses to use those abilities rather than on how many cases of Scotch his or her great-grandfather had sold, or how many barrels of oil his or her grandfather had pumped, or how many cannons and horsemen his or her ancestors had 500 years ago. But Kurt couldn't get it.

As Kurt's father continued to wait, a series of thoughts came to him of an aspect of the new world order that might actually help Kurt quite a bit and might help him get with the program, so to speak. Kurt's father started reciting in his mind what he knew about how business now worked: 'Businesses aren't funded and controlled by investors any more, meaning that they're not controlled by people sitting on the sidelines loudly reciting their singular mantra: "Give us more money, now! Give us more money, now!" Instead, they are controlled by the people who started the business and who are personally, rather than financially, invested in it.

'Now, to start a business, a person or group of people submits a proposal for a startup package that includes facilities, credits for equipment and raw materials, and the authority to recruit employees (who would still be paid based on their current level, of course). Proposals are approved based on the current societal need for what is being proposed, the capabilities of the proposing person or team, and the business, technological, and ecological quality of what is being proposed. In the case of first-time proposers, all but the very last of these, ecological quality, are generally interpreted loosely. In principal, when the people who start a business pass on or are otherwise unable to continue it or uninterested in continuing it, it can be transferred to other people who propose to keep running it. But, in practice, it's much more common for the resources of the business to be returned for others to use in starting new businesses.

'This could seem inefficient,' Kurt's father continued to think to himself, 'because it means businesses come and go pretty quickly, so there's no long-term continuity or experience base. That's partly true. But virtually any winning proposal of greater than one person includes one or more experienced people to act as mentors. Also, savvy customers are able to quickly separate the wheat from the chaff. So, businesses that aren't cutting it don't last very long. Since people no longer depend on their businesses for their survival, it's not that big a deal for a business to fail now. People simply move on to something else. There is a bit of a blow to the ego for those who started the business, though. So, there's a bit of a self-selection effect. People who are unlikely to be good at running a business are unlikely to try to start one (although there are definite exceptions, often punctuated by dismal failures).

'A big benefit of relatively short lived businesses is that they can be flexible. Businesses can be created to provide goods and services to meet market needs rather than long-lived businesses trying to create markets to force their goods and services into. The first of these is far kinder to the environment because resources get used because they need to be used rather than, for example, because a mega car company needs to push several million vehicles on the public a year to stay alive (when there were mega car companies, that is).'

Kurt came back from the bathroom and as he was sitting back down his father said, "I was just thinking, maybe your current job isn't the right fit for you. Maybe the chemistry just isn't quite right. I think you should consider starting your own research and development business."

"Dad, if you weren't my father I'd call that a stupid idea. But you are, so I'll just call it crazy. I just got downgraded 3 levels in two years. Do you really think I'd be approved for a startup package?"

Kurt's father remembered why he didn't like having his son around that much. But he still loved him as his son and tolerated him, because that's what fathers do – in the past and in the present and in the future.

"Son," Kurt's father said, "you are the most cynical individual I have ever met." Then he went on with his story.

Chapter 21
(The Present)

Lacey didn't come back to Chase's for three nights. The first night, Chase didn't think much of it, although he worried a little that he might have offended her in some way, like by inviting her to stay over after knowing her for such a short time. The second night, his worry started to take firmer hold of him and he started kicking himself for being such a jerk. He tried to tell himself that he actually hadn't been much of a jerk, but he had trouble believing himself. He thought of calling her. But he decided no, he'd give it another day or two. The third night, he was deeply relieved when he answered the door and Lacey was standing there. But he could tell right away something was wrong. "What's the matter?" he asked.

"It's my father," Lacey answered.

"What happened, did he take a turn for the worse?"

"No, Chase," Lacey answered. "My father died last night." Chase could tell that Lacey was trying hard to stay composed. A tear rolled down her cheek anyway.

Chase took Lacey in his arms and held her. "I'm really sorry," he said. Lacey cried.

"Come in," Chase said. Chase kept his arm around Lacey to offer her support, both physical and emotional. Chase guided Lacey to his large chocolate-brown couch and they sat down. "Tell me what happened."

"There's not much to tell. The doctors said his liver just gave out completely. They weren't expecting that, at this point. But they said his liver must have been farther gone than they realized when they brought him in."

"I'm really sorry," Chase said again. They sat on the couch for a long time. Lacey rested her head on Chase's shoulder. She sniffled every now and then, but was otherwise quiet. In a spontaneous moment, Chase gave Lacey a kiss full on her lips. The kiss was inspired more by compassion than passion. But it could have turned passionate given even a little time. Lacey returned the kiss for a brief moment, but then she pulled away.

"I'm really sorry," Chase said a third time. "The last thing you need is a lame guy hitting on you right now."

"It's okay. I know you pretty much mean well. And you're not looking lame right at the moment, by the way," Lacey said looking down at Chase's lap. She smiled a little bit, in spite of situation. Chase turned a little red and covered himself with a pillow from the couch. They sat there for several more minutes.

Chase said, "So, do you want to tell me about your father?"

"Yeah, I guess that might help. You already know the first thing I know, which is that he lost his hand in Vietnam. He hardly ever talked about anything before that – you know, like his childhood or whatever. Both his parents died way before I was born. So, I didn't know either of them. When I was young, I didn't see much of him. Up until I was about five, he was working on his PhD. So, then I basically never saw him. After that, he spent most of his time working. I think he was overcompensating a bit because he had a late start due to his time in the service. When I did see him during that time, he didn't talk to me much. He stayed pretty distant. Actually, though, I guess that's not unlike a lot of fathers, from what people have told me. That all changed when my mother was killed."

"Wait, before you go on, what was your mother like?"

Lacey smiled. "My mother was a wonderful, caring, beautiful woman. Those are the memories of a young girl, since my mother was killed when I was twelve. So, they may be a little biased. But I don't think so. My mother walked and talked like she had a noble upbringing, like she was a princess or something. I used to imagine her living in a castle when she was a girl, with a moat and everything. Silly, I know, but that's what I used to imagine. I never knew her parents.   But I imagined them to be part of the American aristocracy. I really liked that.

"My mother was a slender woman. She had wavy dark hair with a faint vanilla scent and dark almond eyes. I remember that really well because she used to spend a lot of time holding me and when she wasn't holding me, she was watching me. I think she was trying to make up for my father some. Or maybe she was using me as a comfort from him; you know, holding onto me like a little kid might hold onto a baby blanket. I'm not sure which. Anyway, she used to say, 'Everything he's doing, he's doing for us, sweetheart; really, he is,' like she was trying to convince herself as much as me.

"In a way, I think my father scared my mother. I don't think he ever hurt her or anything. But he could be very intense sometimes. He'd get in these extremely dark moods, moping around the house doing little more than grunting when my mother would try to say something to him. In hindsight, I'm sure he was being tormented by demons from his past – maybe from his childhood, maybe from Vietnam, whatever; I don't know.   Luckily for my mother and me, I guess, he internalized his struggles rather than externalizing them. He tore himself up rather than us. But, like I said, we didn't have to deal with that too often because he wasn't home very much.

"All that changed when my mother was killed. Her death really freaked my father out. It's like it was his own private little shock treatment and it totally changed him. I think my father realized that I was all he had left. So, I became his project, his reason for living. He became very attentive and very protective. He used to come home from work as soon as his last class was over instead of staying at his office until all hours of the night doing whatever it is he used to do there. Instead of moping around the house, he spent hours teaching me self defense and other things he learned in his Airborne Ranger training. As an Airborne Ranger, his whole mission in Vietnam was to get dropped from airplanes behind enemy lines, take out key enemy positions, and fight his way back to safety. No wonder he was intense, right? Anyway, so he taught me all this stuff and kept telling me to take it seriously because I might need it one day. So, like, if I wanted to, I could take you out in about half a second. So, you better not try to kiss me again."

A light poke in the ribs let Chase know not to take that threat seriously. "Yeah, I guess I better watch myself. Down, boy," he said, pointing at his pillow-covered lap. "So, it didn't seem a little odd to you that your father was teaching you all this stuff?"

"Hey, I was twelve and my mother's near constant attention kept me from having many friends. So, what the hell did I know? I'd been taking Taekwondo for a few years by then, anyway. So, learning fighting stuff seemed natural enough.

"The training went on for about four years until either I 'graduated', or my father became less freaked out about my mother's death, or he finally realized I actually needed a life, or some combination of all of those. After that, luckily, I was finally free of insanely overbearing parents and had a chance to develop a little more normally, leading to the mature, well adjusted woman sitting next to you."

"Yeah, well, we'll withhold judgment on that just a little longer," said Chase. That earned him a slightly sharper poke in the ribs. "What do you do now? I don't even know."

"I'm about to graduate from Caltech," Lacey answered bursting into tears. She was just realizing that, even if she were able to get through her classes with all that was going on, her father wouldn't be at her graduation.

"I'm really sorry," Chase said a final time. Lacey put her head on Chase's shoulder again and they just sat.

After several minutes, Lacey continued, "When my training, or whatever you want to call it, ended, my father didn't sink back into his morose slugfest with his demons. Instead, he traded that slugfest in for the slugfest with God I was talking about the last time I was here.   And he traded me in as his project for his crusade."

Chapter 22
(The Present)

"This is your father's *fix the world* crusade?" Chase asked.

"Yeah, that's right," answered Lacey, "his *fix the world* crusade. As I already pretty much said, if you've been paying attention, it started about 6 years ago. It started off pretty slow, and I'm not sure whether he was really meaning to start a long term thing at the beginning. He started by arranging to speak in the quad area on your campus where they hold rallies sometimes. You know where I'm talking about, right?"

"Yeah, I know where you're talking about. Over kind of by Ackerman Union."

"Yeah, I guess. Anyway, he arranged to speak there and he was pretty successful. People seemed to really buy into what he was saying."

"What was he saying?" Chase asked.

"I don't really remember very well. He took me, but I was more interested in checking out cute college guys than listening to what my father was talking about. I'd just been released from many years in the parental cage, you know. But it seems to me he was talking about the unfairness of the huge disparity of wealth between the haves and the have nots. Like the crap you were talking about when you were telling me about Jill Bates last time I was here. I remember there was quite a bit of clapping and all, like people were really into what he was saying. That's not too surprising for a bunch of idealistic college students – even rich ones. But, as time went on, he started catching the attention of the establishment, so to speak, in good ways and bad ways.

"With the success of his first speech, he scheduled more speeches and more and more people came. He changed up what he talked about. But most of it revolved around the often unfair and sometimes brutal ways that both people and our earth are treated. This is the kind of thing that caught the attention of the establishment in a good way. People who have a genuine caring for other people and the earth were attracted to what he was saying. He started being invited to evening programs at churches and stuff like that.

"But he also talked about how our political and economic systems support and even encourage the often unfair and sometimes brutal ways that people and the earth are treated. That's what started catching the attention of the establishment in a bad way. He even went so far as to say our democratic system is flawed. He said it almost always forces us down a path of mediocrity. The reason is that we can't choose the best at something, because one person's best is another person's worst. For example, the best candidate to preserve the earth would likely be the worst to preserve corporate profit. The best candidate to save people by providing reasonable healthcare to all would probably be the worst at saving the astronomical profits of the medical industry. Are you starting to sense a trend here?"

"Yeah, I'm getting it," Chase answered. "And I kind of see your father's point. But what's the alternative, a dictator?"

"No. That would be crazy even for my father. He had in mind that the people would still elect their leaders. But, instead of the richly funded beauty contests that we call elections now, the people would select their leaders from a pool of professional governors who would actually be trained and qualified to govern and who, once admitted to the pool, would be supported comfortably, but not extravagantly, for life. That way, they wouldn't need to worry about losing their livelihood as punishment for making unpopular, but otherwise necessary, decisions. Oh, and once admitted to the pool, a professional governor wouldn't be able to receive any other compensation of any kind, monetary, material, or service-related, from anywhere, also for life. So, becoming a governor would mean making a lifelong commitment to public service."

"So, I guess you paid some attention, after all," said Chase.

"Yeah, I started paying attention after a while. Another thing about the mediocre path that democracy leads us down, by the way, is that it makes many things of importance move at glacial speeds. That was becoming a huge concern of my father's. He was becoming obsessed with the idea that we're running out of time, that we're killing our life-sustaining earth faster than we're fixing it and that we're fast approaching the point of no return."

"That sounds pretty heavy," said Chase. "But quite a few people are clanging the warning bells these days. What was drawing people to your father? Was it his message, or was it him?"

"I think it was a little of both. As I've said before, he was intense. He channeled that into his passionate commitment to his cause and it came through and it drew people to him. But I think he would say ... sorry, would *have said*, that in a way he was in the right place at the right time. More and more individuals are seeing the light and, as they do, society is evolving, becoming slightly more mature, if you will. People are starting to realize that, as the world gets smaller and smaller, we need to treat each other and our earth better. So, society is becoming more receptive to my father's message. Twenty years ago, even ten years ago, he would have been talking to himself, the sidewalks, and a few members of the fringe element over there by Ackerman Union. That's what he would have said, anyway.

"Somewhat ironically, it was the part of my father's message that was catching the attention of the establishment in a bad way that was probably furthering his cause the most, because it was drawing the press. You can say how we should save the earth and feed the hungry and that kind of stuff all day long and the press doesn't really give much of a shit. But if a relatively prominent person says out loud that our democracy just might semi-suck and there just might be a better way and more than a few people seem to listen, wham – they're on you like bees on honey. You know, controversy sells newspapers and air time. There's a rumor that the coverage was going national at my father's next rally. That's probably why they killed –"

Lacey bolted straight upright, startling Chase enough to make his heart skip a beat. "Chase!" she said excitedly, even frantically, "Get me into the Pinky site!"

Chase realized that it would have been futile to remind Lacey that every time he hacked into the Pinky site he risked being caught at worst or having his way in blocked at best. So, he said, "Okay. It'll take a few minutes." Chase walked over to his computer and started doing his magic. A few minutes later, he said, "Okay, you're in. Don't take too long."

Lacey sat down at Chase's computer and started to explore. She saw what Chase meant about the site being more operational than biographical. There were scads of case files, but not much information about the Pinkies themselves, probably on purpose. After a few minutes, she found what she was looking for and breathed a long and low, "Holy fucking shit." Five weeks ago to the day, the following message had been transmitted to the intracranial receiver of a Pinky named Dex:

TARGET: Dr. Randal Dean Howard, professor
of Political Science, University of California,
Los Angeles; PRIORITY: High; MODE: Covert.
– REPEAT –
TARGET: Dr. Randal Dean Howard, professor
of Political Science, University of California,
Los Angeles; PRIORITY: High; MODE: Covert.

Lacey would learn later that the mode was almost always covert, but right then it didn't matter. Lacey closed the screen and began to cry.

Chase walked over and put his hand on Lacey's shoulder. "What is it?" he asked. "What did you find?"

"Nothing," Lacey sobbed. "I didn't find anything. I was just thinking of my dad." It was unusual for Lacey to lie like that. But she had things she needed to sort out.

Chapter 23
(The Present)

For the next few days, Chase and Lacey didn't see too much of each other. Lacey didn't have any relatives (that she knew of, anyway). So, it fell on her shoulders to take care of her father's affairs, including clearing out his university office, arranging his memorial service, arranging his burial, and everything else that goes along with a person being there one day and gone the next. The one day that Lacey did stop by, she asked Chase if he would accompany her to her father's service the following Tuesday at 3:00 PM. He said that he would be honored.

When Tuesday came around, Chase put on the gray pinstripe suit that he had worn once before, to his brother's wedding, and the shoes that looked nice, but pinched his feet. Lacey picked him up in her Beemer and they drove to the Church of Saint Peter Martyr. The service was pretty much normal. Lacey's father's body wasn't present, which is what made it a memorial service rather than a funeral. But there were a lot of pictures of him from about the time he married Lacey's mother and onward – Lacey couldn't find any earlier pictures. The priest did a good job with the homily and an okay job saying a few words about him, even though he didn't know him very well – or actually at all, the truth be known. A few other people stood up and said a few words when invited to do so. Lacey wanted to, but she didn't. She didn't think she'd be able to hold it together.

The one thing that made the service stand out, if anything did, was the number of people there. The church could easily seat 700 and it was filled to overflowing. It may have been paranoia on Lacey's part, but she thought some of the people looked a bit shady. She wondered for a moment if Dex, her father's killer, was there. But then she thought, *No, why would he be*, and didn't think about it again. But Dex was there and he didn't look a bit shady. In fact, he was one of the more normal looking people at the service. If Lacey had thought about it, which of course she had no reason to, she probably would have thought he was one of her father's colleagues when he shook her hand after the service and offered his condolences.

Chapter 24
(The Present)

After her father's memorial service, Lacey tried to live at home and carry on with her life as usual. But she found herself getting lonely and the empty house was giving her the creeps. So, she ended up spending more and more time over at Chase's. She was still conflicted about whether to ask him what she wanted to. After a few days, she realized that time was getting short and decided that she had to either do it and be done with it, or decide once and for all not to.

Lacey took the remote, paused the movie they were watching, and said, "So, Chase, I've been trying to decide whether to ask you to do something."

"Oh, really?" said Chase. "Wait, let me guess, you've fallen deeply and madly in love with me and you want to have my baby." Although he had thought about it many times, he hadn't tried to hit on Lacey again since his spontaneous attempt the night her father died, partly because he knew she was mourning his loss and partly because he was thinking that his lust might be metamorphosizing into love and so, somewhat ironically, he wanted to wait.

"Am I going to have to kick your ass so early in our friendship? Because, I would take no pleasure in it. But I'll do it if I have to."

"Whoa, I'm shaking in my boots," Chase said and then glanced at his feet. "Well, I'm shaking in my slippers, anyway. Okay, I give up. What do you want to ask me?"

"My father's next rally was scheduled for the middle of March, so in about three weeks. If that's canceled, my father's movement dies along with him. If someone takes his place, though, it has at least the chance of surviving. When my father spoke your name on his deathbed, I thought it was because of your brilliant computer skills, which have admittedly started to be useful. But now I think that at least part of what he wanted was for you to take his place in his crusade. So, the question is, would you take my father's place at his next rally?"

"Wait, let me get this straight, you think your father was killed for his cause and now you want me to try to carry it on?"

Lacey didn't bother saying that she didn't *think* her father was killed for his cause, she *knew* her father was killed for his cause. "I know it's a huge thing to ask," she answered. "That's why I've worried so much about whether to ask you. But I think my father's movement was actually starting to make a difference. I think that's why they killed him. If his movement ends, they win."

"They win, huh? Is this about helping people or about vengeance?"

Lacey thought about it for a few moments. "Truthfully," she said, "I think it's some of both. But you can do it just for the helping people part. You won't be doing it alone. I'll be with you every step of the way. I'll do the administrative parts, like letting my father's core supporters know what's going on, confirming the venue, getting out the advertising, making sure the press remembers it, and so on. I found my father's file on the rally. So, I know who I need to contact. I know some of the people, anyway. And, also, I think I'll be able to protect you, if I need to." She thought to herself that her father might be right – she might need the "Airborne Ranger" training that he gave her one day. Also, she could use the Pinky site for Chase threat alerts.

"One minute you're kicking my ass and the next minute you're protecting me? You really have a knack for boosting a guy's ego," Chase said half seriously.

Normally, Lacey would have smiled and said something sarcastic, like, "*Aw, did I hurt the poor little girl's feelings?*" But she didn't. Instead, she said, "Chase, this is serious. Will you do it?"

Chase realized that what he was about to say would likely be evidence of clinical insanity. But he also realized at that moment that his lust for Lacey had, in fact, metamorphosized into love. "Yes, I'll do it," he said.

And the timer ticked on...

Chapter 25
(The Future)

The doorbell rang and, as he got up to answer it, Kurt's father said, "That's probably Uncle Greg and Aunt Gail."

"Oh, swell," Kurt said under his breath. If Kurt's father heard that, he ignored it.

"Kurt's here. Come in and say hi," Kurt's father said as he led Uncle Greg and Aunt Gail into the kitchen and motioned to them to sit down at the polished chrome table.

"Oh look, Dear, Kurt's here," said Uncle Greg, taking a seat. "How are you, young man?"

"Oh, I'm not so bad. I hear you were approved for a third. Congratulations," Kurt said, showing that he wasn't completely lacking in all social graces.

"Yes, thank you," said Aunt Gail. "We're very excited!"

"So, it doesn't bother you that the government actually needs to approve your having a baby?" Kurt said, showing that he was lacking in most social graces.

"No, it doesn't bother us at all," Uncle Greg said, taking the question in stride. "We, along with most people on the planet, realize that the earth cannot sustain unlimited population growth and we're willing to accept controls to prevent that. The controls are fair, you know."

"They're God damned invasive is what they are!" said Kurt, his ever-simmering anger starting to bubble up.

"Settle down, Kurt," said his father.

"No, it's okay," said Uncle Greg, "I don't mind going a couple of rounds with my old friend Kurt. So, is that what you talked about at your Indie meeting at your house the other night? I hear there were a lot of people there."

"How did you know about that?" Kurt asked, slightly taken aback.

"It's a small world, Kurt, and news tends to travel fast. One of my students was there and she told me you were ranting about the unfairness of men being rationed to two fertilizations and women being rationed to two fertilizations – unless you apply and your number comes up in the third lottery, as Aunt Gail's and mine did, of course. My student also said you were going on and on about how the rationing shouldn't be enforced by installing birth control devices in every pre-pubescent boy and girl on the planet."

"Yeah, that really sucks!" said Kurt. "I'm a reasonably smart guy. I realize that our small planet can't support limitless life. But can't people be trusted to take responsibility for that themselves? Should people really need to go to the Reproductive Containment Agency to have their reproductive organs turned on when they want to have a baby? Should women really need to be scanned every two months to make sure there hasn't been an accident?"

Uncle Greg responded, "You and Jennifer just went to the RCA yourselves, didn't you? So, you know first-hand that it takes about five minutes for the RC Specialist to check that you're both eligible and then enter the codes that get transmitted to your birth control devices to 'turn you on', as you put it. No fuss, no muss. And you also know that reading a woman's hormone sensor is simply a matter of walking through one of the scanners that are all over the place. In fact, a woman would have to go out of her way *not* to walk through a scanner several times a month. Frequent scanning is needed so that a woman can terminate an 'accident' in her first trimester, if that's what she feels is right. You know no one is forced to do that, although it's strongly recommended for the good of the earth. It doesn't matter these days, anyway, though. There hasn't been an 'accident' in nearly twenty years."

"Yeah, nearly twenty years! So again I ask, can't people be trusted to take responsibility for population control themselves?"

"Kurt, now that major religions of the world have stopped ramming the 'be fruitful and multiply' message down their followers' throats, asking people to be responsible for population control would have a better chance of working. But, the urge to reproduce is probably the strongest physical urge there is for a woman and the urge to practice reproducing is probably the strongest physical urge there is for a man. These days, most people reach the maturity to control those urges and be responsible in both reproducing and practicing – although, even with that maturity, it's very hard sometimes. But to reach that maturity level, everyone needs to pass through the tumultuous, often irrational, sometimes nearly uncontrollable years of adolescence. For that reason alone, even these days the built-in birth control makes sense."

"You know, Uncle Greg," said Kurt, certain that he had found a chink in his pretend uncle's otherwise seamless moral armor, "that 'urge to reproduce' and 'urge to practice reproducing' language sounds pretty sexist coming from a socially enlightened man like you."

"For a smart guy, you can be pretty naïve sometimes, Kurt," responded Uncle Greg. "No matter how equally society treats the genders, men and women will still be different. It's simple biology. As long as men are men and women are women, their bodies will be different, they will have different reproductive functions, and they will be driven by different hormones. I, personally, wouldn't like it any other way."

"Yeah, I guess I see what you mean. Never mind about that, then," Kurt said, annoyed that he had derailed his main point. Trying to recover it, he said as forcefully as he could without yelling, "What reproductive control all comes down to is that it is yet another example of my individual rights being greatly limited by society. If I want to have three babies, or four babies, or ten babies, I should be able to and I shouldn't need to get society's permission."

"Kurt, luckily for the earth and everyone on it, you are in the small minority – as much as you're trying to change that. But that brings up a point that you might not quite get yet. This is really important, so listen carefully. Like almost everyone these days, Aunt Gail and I haven't waited to have a third child because it's a *rule* or the *law*. We've waited until now because the earth could not support another child of ours. Now it can. Get it? Like almost everyone these days, we don't need external rules or laws. We do our very best to live in synchronicity with the earth and with all of its inhabitants. In short, we try very hard to do what makes global sense."

"Yeah, well, anyway, I have to net Jennifer to let her know I'm running very late. Congratulations again. Although it's probably hard to tell, I really am happy for you."

"Thanks, Kurt," said Aunt Gail. Kurt headed into his old room for a little privacy. When he returned, the talk was about whether Aunt Gail and Uncle Greg were going to renew their coupling contract for another 21 years which, of course, they were. As people lived longer and longer, marriage-for-life was getting rarer and rarer. It was more common for people to use a twenty-one year coupling contract when they were going to have a baby, thereby becoming child-mates. Interestingly, this made it dramatically more likely that a couple would stay committed through the raising of a child than the old marriage-for-life way did. Kurt's father was asking if they were going to have another ceremony.

"Not a big one," Aunt Gail said. "When Jill was conceived, I had my big beautiful ceremony with gowns, tuxedoes, flowers, cake, and dancing. This time, we'll probably have a more modest ceremony, like we did with Nathan, with family and close friends. You'll be there, won't you?"

"Of course," said Kurt's father.

"And you and Jennifer, Kurt?" asked Aunt Gail as she saw him come back into the room.

Kurt wanted to say, *"I'm pretty sure we'll be busy that day."* But, instead, he said, "We wouldn't miss it."

With that, Uncle Greg and Aunt Gail said their goodbyes, Kurt and his father sat back down at the table, and Kurt's father went on with his story.

Chapter 26
(The Present)

Lacey did a good job preparing things for what had turned into Chase's rally. She had confirmed the venue (the same place on the UCLA campus that her father had held his first rally) along with all the loudspeakers, microphones, and other equipment that went along with it. She had gotten the word out and as a result a lot of people had shown up, partly as a tribute to her father and partly out of curiosity. Probably for the second of these reasons, there were at least two news crews there, too.

Lacey got up on the podium first and the crowd quieted down. She spent a moment surveying the hundreds of faces and two TV cameras spread over a large grassy field that sloped gently down away from the podium that stood in a corner of the field. She had seen many of the faces before at her father's previous rallies. Many of the faces belonged to college students. But there was a generous sprinkling of older faces in the crowd too. She spent another brief moment looking at the buildings surrounding the field, including a large library, student union, and classroom building. Then she said, "Good afternoon. Thank you all for coming out today. As some of you know, I'm Lacey Howard, Randy Howard's daughter. As I'm sure all of you know, my father passed away a little over a month ago. If you don't mind, let's have a few moments of silence in my father's memory." The crowd went respectfully silent for about half a minute. Then someone started clapping and the crowd joined in leading to spirited applause.

Lacey smiled broadly and motioned the crowd to quiet down. "Thank you," she said. "Thank you. I'm sure my father would have appreciated that. Now I'd like to introduce someone to you. This person has ideas very similar to my father's. Similar enough, in fact, that when my father was sick and realized he might not make it, he handpicked this person to carry on for him. Please let me introduce Chase Hancock."

Chase walked onto the podium to polite applause. Even though it wasn't a hot day, nervousness formed beads of sweat on his forehead. "Thank you," he said. "I'm a Computer Science major and I'd like to ask you a question that I get asked quite often. How many computer engineers does it take to change a light bulb?" He paused a moment. "None, they blame the electrical engineers and make them change it." There were a few chuckles, mainly from engineering students, but mostly a lot of "oh, brothers" and "awe, jeeses" along with thoughts of, *I gave up my afternoon for this guy?*

The bombed joke had an interesting effect on Chase. It made him think, *Hmm, it can't get any worse than this; so, what the hell...* So, instead of increasing his nervousness, it dissolved it, replacing it with complete calm. With his newfound calmness and a newfound confidence that went along with it, he said, "Okay, let's get one thing straight. As individuals, people are fundamentally good." This brought another round of polite applause. "Unfortunately, there are many things that can corrupt that fundamental goodness – severe hunger, for example. Of course, then we'd have to argue about whether it's bad to steal a loaf of bread to feed your starving child. But let's not go there right now. As another example, some people say power corrupts. I don't think that has to be true, though.

"Something that does corrupt basic goodness, or at least supports the corruption, is the formation of organizations. The reason for this is simple – organizations dilute one of the most powerful enforcers of good there is: *guilt*. 'I didn't want to lay off the thousand mothers and fathers with children to feed,' the manager can say, 'I was forced to by the organization.' 'It's not my fault I murdered a man today,' the soldier can say, 'the organization made me.' 'I didn't decide to increase military spending and decrease education spending,' the senator can say with a wink, 'the organization did.'" The crowd was starting to warm up to Chase.

"The most common example of this is, of course, the corporation. Myriads of sins are committed by corporations so individuals can remain guilt free. If an individual ends up having a twinge of guilt, he or she can go to the corporate confessional and get reminded to say ten 'I need this jobs', say ten 'Hail moneys', promise never to do it again, and be forgiven."

From there, Chase jumped into railing against the huge differences in wealth between the rich and the poor, like he had talked to Lacey about. Like how it doesn't make any sense for some people to make millions of dollars a year while other people live in refrigerator boxes. He went on for about an hour, speaking from the notes that he had studiously prepared some times and improvising at other times. He peppered his talk liberally with what became his catch phrase: "We have to find a better way!"

After his rocky start, Chase ended up being surprisingly charismatic. By the time he was done, his event had the feeling of a political rally for a popular candidate. The crowd seemed to really love him.

When reporting on his rally, the press focused more on Chase's appeal and the crowd's reaction to him than on his message, turning him into a minor celebrity. He even landed interviews on a couple of national morning news shows. On those, he banged his "We have to find a better way!" gong, which was starting to cause quite a stir.

Even the conservative press fanned the flames. Dash Lamebutt, the popular conservative talk radio host, branded Chase as the latest flake from the state of fruits and nuts. "How can Mr. Hancock be so naïve to say that people are fundamentally good," he asked his listeners, "when any rational person knows that all people are born in sin? Next, he'll probably be asking us to love our neighbors as ourselves. What a pansy-assed crackpot!" Even Mr. Lamebutt's staunchest supporters weren't sure whether he was just being sarcastic with the "love our neighbors as ourselves" crack, or whether he was back to abusing prescription drugs, or whether he had finally lost his tenuous grasp on reality and been sucked into his self-constructed vortex of misrepresentations, fabrications, and deceptions. In a few weeks, nobody would care, though, not even Mr. Lamebutt's staunchest supporters.

Not wanting to lose Chase's momentum, Lacey scheduled another rally for two weeks after the first one.

Chapter 27
(The Present)

The night of Chase's first rally, he and Lacey did several things they had never done before. They bought a bottle of champagne, took what had become their customary seats on the large chocolate-brown couch that dominated Chase's living room, and celebrated the success of the rally. Normally, neither of them drank very much. So, it didn't take much to get them tipsy. They spent time making small talk and being generally happier than either of them had been in quite some time. If either of them had thought about it, which they didn't, they would have realized that, although the alcohol amplified the happiness, the underlying cause was each other.

Part way into the evening, Chase looked deeply into Lacey's eyes and she looked deeply back. Chase leaned in to kiss Lacey and she didn't pull away. She knew she should have, but she didn't. Chase pulled her strongly into his arms and kissed her full on the lips and she kissed back. He explored with his tongue and so did she. He tentatively caressed her breast through her top and bra and she didn't stop him. Instead, she kissed him a little harder. Chase picked Lacey up and carried her to his room and lay her down on his bed. He loosened her shorts and slipped his hand in, finding her womanhead. He rubbed it, starting gently and slowly, but then more firmly and quickly as she started moaning slightly and straining up against his fingers.

Chase took off his shorts and his tighty-whiteys with the 34 inch waste and then Lacey's shorts and her light-pink panties. He moved between her legs and Lacey gasped just a bit as he entered her. It wasn't that she wasn't ready; she was, with her natural moisture in plentiful abundance. It was that Chase was a little bigger than she expected. She was pleased that her thorough research hadn't revealed everything. But then she didn't think about her research for a while.

Chase's thrusting and Lacey's responses started slowly, but then built into a frenzied back-arching crescendo that took them both to levels of ecstasy neither had known before.

As Chase rolled off panting, Lacey said, "Wow, that was fantastic!"

"You seem surprised," Chase said.

"No, no, I'm not surprised," she said. But she was.

"I'm a little bit surprised," said Chase. "It's never been like that for me before. But I don't think it's me. I think it's more you. I think you've made me better than I used to be – in many ways, actually."

"That's an amazingly vulnerable thing for a man to say," said Lacey.

"Is it?" Chase asked.

"Yeah, it is," Lacey answered and kissed him gently on the cheek. In this moment of surrender, this fleeting moment of weakness that was one of the very few in her life, Lacey was afraid she had fallen in love with Chase. She knew she shouldn't have, but she did. She would remember this moment for the rest of her life.

"So, you really think I'm a man?" Chase asked, feeling a wave of pride pass through him.

"Yeah, I do," answered Lacey. And she did.

Chapter 28
(The Present)

Because of what had happened to her father and because of Chase's quick success, Lacey was afraid the same thing might happen to him. So, a couple of days before his next rally, Lacey convinced him to show her how to hack into the Pinky site. She promised to use it very sparingly. The night before the rally, she logged in and, sure enough, she found what she expected. The following had been transmitted to the intracranial receiver of Dex, the same Pinky who had killed her father:

> TARGET: Chase Arthur Hancock, student,
> University of California, Los Angeles;
> PRIORITY: Imperative; MODE: Assassination.
> – REPEAT –
> TARGET: Chase Arthur Hancock, student,
> University of California, Los Angeles;
> PRIORITY: Imperative; MODE: Assassination.

Lacey would learn later that the mode *Assassination* had only been used a few times before and would be astonished at the names attached to it. Normally, Pinkies were instructed to make their hits look like accidents and were given quite a bit of latitude in their methods. But every now and then, an explicit example needed to be made. Chase, it seemed, needed to be such an example.

Since Lacey had expected this message, she had thought quite a bit about what to do about it. She knew that if she canceled the rally due to this threat, there would never be another one because if there ever was, she would find the same message again. So, at this point, for her father's and now Chase's movement, it was do or die. Unfortunately for Chase, it was likely to be do *and* die. She had decided that she must let the rally go on and that she MUST protect Chase.

Lacey knew that for maximum effect the assassination would happen at Chase's rally and she knew that for maximum effect it would be done with a gun. So, she had gone to her father's weapons stash, that she knew about from her father's training, and found what she needed. She knew the only advantage she would have over Dex would be that he would not be expecting her.

Chapter 29
(The Present)

As he was getting out of his car, Dex had to pause because he was hearing a message in his head: "Target: Chase Arthur Hancock, student, University of California, Los Angeles; priority: Imperative; mode: Assassination. – Repeat – Target: Chase Arthur Hancock, student, University of California, Los Angeles; Priority: Imperative; Mode: Assassination." The first time he heard a message in his head, when he was little more than a boy, it had seemed kind of weird – kind of crazy weird like when crazy people hear voices in their heads. But, after fifteen years, it now seemed completely natural. In fact, now-a-days, if he didn't have to memorize every word of the message, he wouldn't even bother slowing down. But he did, because messages were never repeated and he was NEVER to contact his handlers. He had a phone number, just in case. But he wasn't even sure it worked, because he had never tried it.

Dex didn't have trouble memorizing every word of messages because he was very smart. Along with his smarts, he had the classic good looks that would normally carry a man far, even under the most modest of circumstances. If he hadn't fled his physically abusive father when he was thirteen, he probably would have become a brain surgeon or a rocket scientist or some such thing. But he did flee his physically abusive father when he was thirteen. So, instead, he became part of the over-abundant teenage runaway population and then was recruited to be one of the five most cunning, creative, ruthless killers on the planet, ever.

Dex also didn't have trouble memorizing every word of messages because they all had the same format and used the same code words. They started with the target's name and uniquely identifying information. It would be a waste to take the wrong target out because a job generally took quite a bit of planning and preparation and, if you took out the wrong target, you'd just be ordered to turn around and take out the right one. That almost never happened.

Then came the priority, that was either *Low* (do these at your convenience), *Medium* (important, but if these take a while, no worries), *High* (these should be your top priorities, unless there's an *Imperative*), or *Imperative* (drop everything else and do this one as close to immediately as feasible). Pinkies generally had only one job working at any given time. But there were occasional busy spells when a Pinky could have two or three or even four jobs working.

Next was the mode: *Covert* (make it look like an accident – this was the norm and part of the reason a job generally took quite a bit of planning and preparation), *Overt* (it's okay if it looks like a murder or some such thing), *Hit* (make it look like the mob), *Assassination* (make it a murder with a message, usually political), and *Pinky* (you're taking out one of your own). This last one had only been used once.

Finally, there was occasionally a location given. But this was unusual.

Since Dex was very smart, he wasn't at all surprised that the name of his latest target was Chase Hancock or that the mode was *Assassination*. Remarkably, Hancock had recovered Randy Howard's movement and built on it impressively in just a few weeks. It was time to send a message to shit-disturbers like him: "You can't threaten the status quo and get away with it!" At least that's what Dex figured his handlers thought. He rarely troubled himself with such matters.

Since the priority for Chase Hancock was *Imperative*, Dex got right on it. He checked when and where Chase's next rally was going to be. He was very familiar with the location because he had checked it over when he was planning Randy Howard's job. But he went over there anyway. As he remembered, there was one building that still had windows that opened. The building had a clear view of where Hancock would be standing. It was about 200 yards away, which was a stretch for a single clean shot. But Dex had handled longer distances. With his bionic eye, aiming at such distances was no problem and his high-powered rifle was nearly an extension of his arm by then, with all the years he had practiced with it (and occasionally used it). He very rarely used a tripod.

Dex went into the class room on the third floor that would give him the best horizontal angle and opened a window about six inches. *Yes, that's perfect*, he thought. *I can stand back a few feet, still see the target, and have the right vertical angle for a clean hit.* He noted that the door didn't lock, but that he could jam a chair under the doorknob to keep a lost student or a custodian from barging in on him. The door had a window, but there was an adequate shade over it. There was also an old style cloudy window above the door. But it was closed and, of course, too high for anyone to see in even if it was open. All that remained was to make sure that a class wouldn't be in session in the room. He checked that on the Internet when he got home. He was good to go...

Chapter 30
(The Present)

As Chase and Lacey were getting in her car to go to his rally, Lacey seemed agitated. "Are you okay?" Chase asked her.

"Yeah, I'm okay," she answered. "It's just nerves, I think. A lot's happened in the past few weeks." There was no sense telling Chase that, unless she was successful against immense odds, she was driving him to his death. No, no sense telling him that at all.

"Yeah," said Chase, "that's for sure."

When they got to the rally, Laccy left Chase at his podium to get his thoughts together. As she left him, she gave him a passionate kiss on the lips and said, "Good luck." She was saying this as much to herself as to him.

"Wow, thanks," Chase said with a big smile.

Lacey went back to her car and got her bag out of her trunk. She had been by the day before to check the place over, and so knew where to look – at the building that still had windows that opened. It was a hot day, so no windows should be open because the air conditioning would be on. But when she looked, sure enough, there was a window on the third floor open about six inches. She walked toward the building, with only a vague idea of what she was going to do. She knew she had a few minutes, because Dex would wait until the rally was in full swing for maximum effect. But not many minutes.

When it was about time for Chase to start, he looked around for Lacey to see if she was going to introduce him. But she didn't seem to be around. *That's odd,* he thought, as he looked out at his large audience. As Chase stepped up onto his podium, there was the equivalent of a movie star's welcome, complete with enthusiastic applause, whistles, and a few people calling out his name. "Thank you," he said, motioning the people to quiet down. "Thank you," he said again.

As the crowd started to quiet itself, he said, "Wow, it's been quite a couple of weeks." That livened the clapping again. "The last time I was here," Chase said, talking over the applause, "we talked about how corporations and organizations can turn inherently good people into not so good groups of people. I guess I shouldn't pick on corporations too much. But they do another thing in today's society. They serve as the militaries of the upper class. It's frowned upon these days for the nobles to battle each other with horses or tanks or swords or guns or catapults or cannons, tromping over the fields of the serfs as they please. So, they do it in other ways. These days, you still have your nobles – but now we call them board members, CEOs, CFOs, COOs, etc. You still have your serfs – but now we call them employees. You still have your taxes paid to the nobles – but now we call them profits. You still have your weapons – but now we call them pens and accountants and computers and lobbyists. And you still have the final goal of *killing the enemy* – but now we call it *killing the competition.*

"The nobles of today have done one better than their more violent predecessors, though. They've found a way to have the serfs give them portions of their meager savings to play with, with the promise that the serfs *might* get a return on that money – sometimes that happens and other times it doesn't, right?" The crowd responded energetically, with many people yelling, "Yeah, right!" and many others yelling, "Yeah, sometimes!"

"So, which of these peaceful militaries has been super successful at *killing the competition* lately?" The names of several corporations were yelled out, including the one Chase was looking for – SamsMart.

"Yeah, SamsMart," Chase said. "Is it right for SamsMart to come into an area and build just outside a city limit so they don't have to pay the taxes that support the city and that their competition pays?"

"Hell no!" cried the crowd.

"Is it right for SamsMart to pay people barely livable wages, hire many of their employees part time so they don't have to pay benefits, dangle the many other people who would like a job in front of employees noses to force them to work unpaid overtime, and even instruct them on how to get support from the government, support that you and I pay for?"

"Hell no!" cried the crowd.

"Is it right for SamsMart to dictate to manufacturers what they will make, when they will make it, and what they will be paid?"

"Hell no!" cried the crowd.

"Is it right for SamsMart to put all this together and *kill the competition*, some of which happens to be the stores owned and operated by our brothers and sisters and mothers and fathers and sons and daughters, stores that pay fair wages and offer benefits and actually care about their employees?"

"Hell no!" cried the crowd.

"Is it right that our economic system allows – even supports – this kind of corporate behavior?"

"Hell no!" cried the crowd.

"We have to find a better way!"

"Hell yes!" cried the crowd, applauding wildly and shouting Chase's phrase back at him – "We have to find a better way!"

Chapter 31
(The Present)

When Lacey got to the third floor, she took a pair of slippers out of her bag and put them on. This was so Dex's bionic ear wouldn't hear her stop in front of the classroom with the window open about six inches. Lacey knew which classroom to go to because she had counted windows. This was confirmed because there was only one classroom with the door closed and the shade down.

What Lacey wanted to do was crash through the door and say to Dex, "*This is for killing my father*," like they do in the movies, and then shoot him. But she knew if she was going to do that, she might as well just stick the business end of a .45 in her mouth and pull the trigger, because either would be an equally effective form of suicide.

Lacey tried to peak around the edge of the shade. But she couldn't see anything worth seeing. She looked up at the old style cloudy window above the door and saw that it was closed, but there was a slight crack. So, it probably wasn't latched. That seemed kind of sloppy to Lacey. But then she remembered her single advantage over Dex: he wouldn't be expecting her. Lacey very quietly got a desk from a nearby classroom, set it down in front of the door, and climbed on it. Sure enough, the cloudy window was not latched.

A plan formed in Lacey's mind. All she needed to do was push the window open, locate Dex in the room, aim at the very specific location she needed to shoot her dart, and shoot it, all before he swung his high-powered rifle around, or more likely drew a weapon that he doubtless had close at hand, and shot her. It was kind of like a modern day version of a wild-west quick draw, she thought – she had to be deadly fast and deadly accurate. She had to be particularly accurate with the weapon she had chosen from her father's stash. It was a high powered dart gun containing a dart with an ultra-thin, but ultra-hard and ultra-sharp needle. The dart contained a drug used to stop hearts during cardiac surgeries. The advantages of the drug were it was fast acting and very difficult to detect unless you were looking for it. The disadvantage was the minor detail that the needle had to hit the heart. Lacey cursed herself for choosing that weapon; she would need to get the needle between Dex's ribs. But she had what she had, so she had no choice. She went for it.

Lacey executed her plan flawlessly. She started by holding the dart gun in position right in front of her face. Then, she quickly and forcefully pushed the cloudy window open with her left hand and began moving the dart gun into position at the same time she was locating Dex in the room – he was looking down the barrel of his high-powered rifle with his bionic eye, clearly ready to fire at any moment. He was farther from the open window than she expected. But she still had enough angle to get below his shoulder blade. She quickly but carefully aimed and fired her dart. The dart split Dex's ribs and pierced his heart, injecting its lethal poison. Lacey's father had trained her well.

Even with Lacey's dart in his heart, Dex, with a single motion he must have practiced a million times, let go of the barrel of his rifle, swept his hand across his chest snagging a small revolver from a custom-fit shoulder holster on the way, extended his arm out and slightly back, and got a bead on Lacey before she could move herself even a few inches out of the cloudy window. When Dex saw Lacey's face in the sight of his gun, the faintest hint of recognition and surprise crossed his face. He could have easily put a bullet between Lacey's eyes. But he didn't. Instead, he paused for a fraction of a second, fell forward, and died.

Lacey dropped her bag through the cloudy window and then climbed through herself and dropped to the floor. She pulled her dart out of Dex's back, rubbed what looked like a bleach stick on his shirt to dissolve the small spot of blood from the dart, and sat him up in a chair near the window. She searched him for weapons and threw those (including his revolver and custom-fit shoulder holster), his wallet, and her dart in her bag. She then broke down his high-powered rifle in about five seconds flat and put it in its case, which was on another desk in the classroom, and that went in her bag as well. Finally, she removed the desk that Dex had wedged under the doorknob and climbed on it to push the cloudy window back like it was when she started.

As she was leaving the room to return the desk she had gotten from a nearby classroom, she turned to Dex's lifeless body and said, "That was for killing my father... and, oh yeah, for trying to kill my boyfriend, too." Lacey went back to her car and put her bag back in her trunk.

Chapter 32
(The Present)

As Lacey was returning to the rally from her car, she heard Chase saying, "We have to find a better way! And part of that better way involves the spirit." This caused a moment of dramatic quiet in the crowd followed by an almost universal groan.

"Wait," Chase said. "Wait. I'm not talking about the god of your parents. I'm not talking about God or Jesus or the Holy Spirit or Allah or Vishnu or any other facet of the spirit that's been witnessed, captured, and locked in humanity's death grip. I'm talking about the underlying spirit that's part of all of us and binds us together and would let us live in peace and harmony with each other and the earth, if we would let it." The crowd relaxed a little when they realized that Chase wasn't about to pull a Bible out and start thumping it. There were even some heads that had been shaking *no* a few seconds ago starting to nod *yes*.

"Anyway," said Chase, "I'd like to talk more about the spirit the next time we get together."

Despite the lukewarm reaction to the spirit, as Chase ended his speech he sensed that people were really resonating with what he was saying. He wasn't naïve or arrogant enough to think that the two weeks he had spent in the public light were causing this. He suspected that he, like Dr. Howard before him, was simply giving voice to what poor and wealthy individuals alike, and even some corporations, were starting to realize – that society needed to be guided more by compassion and fairness than by the primitive back-stabbing greed that has changed form but not function since the dawn of humanity. And this was going deeper than the, *"Okay, I'll start a philanthropic foundation to ease my conscience and make people stop saying what a greedy bastard I am"* stage and becoming a fundamental shift in the human psyche – a step into the next level of human maturity, some might say.

The reference to the spirit seemed to confuse the press. The headline for the page-three article on Chase in the local paper the next day said: "California's New Golden Boy: Political Activist or Preacher?" The writer of the article wrestled with this in the context of reporting on Chase's rally and decided that Chase might be a liberal political activist taking a page from the conservative playbook by invoking God to support his cause. (The writer of the article wasn't one of the people resonating with what Chase was saying quite yet.) Toward the end of the article, the writer added a side note about an apparently homeless man who had apparently suffered a heart attack while apparently watching Chase from a third floor classroom across the way. This was barely worth reporting, except for the odd twist that the coroner couldn't confirm the cause of death because the body had been lost somewhere between the third floor classroom and his autopsy table. Another example of incompetence in the medical industry, the writer of the article concluded.

As far as the conservative press was concerned, God or not, Chase was still a flake and they didn't care about the dead homeless guy.

Chapter 33
(The Present)

So as not to let the spirit thing fester for too long and to keep Chase's considerable momentum going (despite the spirit thing), Lacey scheduled a third rally for two weeks after the second one. She checked the Pinky site two days before the third rally and was not surprised to see that Chase had been targeted again, this time by a Pinky named Fred. But she was relieved that Fred apparently had a higher-value target ahead of Chase. The first set of instructions to Fred was:

TARGET: President Achmed Muhammad;
PRIORITY: Imperative; MODE:
Assassination; LOCATION: United Nations.
– REPEAT –
TARGET: President Achmed Muhammad;
PRIORITY: Imperative; MODE:
Assassination; LOCATION: United Nations.

This was followed by instructions for Chase:

TARGET: Chase Arthur Hancock, student,
University of California, Los Angeles;
PRIORITY: High; MODE: Assassination.
– REPEAT –
TARGET: Chase Arthur Hancock, student,
University of California, Los Angeles;
PRIORITY: High; MODE: Assassination.

Lacey knew she had been lucky with Dex at Chase's rally and that she was unlikely to be so lucky a second time. So, if she was going to save Chase from Fred, she was going to have to nip the problem in the bud, so to speak. She looked on the UN website and found that, as luck would have it, Muhammad was addressing the General Assembly on the same afternoon as Chase's rally. So, she told Chase that some unfinished business of her father's had come up, which was pretty much true, and she needed to go to New York for a few days. Chase was pretty upset about that. He said he wanted, even needed, Lacey to be around for his next rally. She was his moral support, he said. But she said she had no choice, so there was nothing they could do about it. So he said okay.

The next day, the day before Chase's rally, Lacey got on a plane and flew to New York City. She took a cab from JFK to a hotel near the UN, checked in, and picked up the package she had FedExed to herself. She spent the following morning checking out the UN and trying to figure how she was going to have any chance of getting Fred. Given the amount of security that would doubtless be surrounding Muhammad, she had no idea how Fred was going to get him, without getting himself caught or more likely killed. But that wasn't her problem. In fact, it might be her solution. If she could be in the right place at the right time, she could shoot the shooter. It was pretty farfetched, but it was the best she had.

Early that afternoon, shortly before Muhammad would be arriving at the UN, Lacey got ready. She put on a slightly-above-the-knee skirt and strapped her plastic but very lethal pistol to her inner thigh as close to her crotch as she could. The idea was that, if she got wanded, the officer would be unlikely to raise her skirt too high and so would hopefully not detect the bullets in her plastic but very lethal gun. (As hard as weapons makers tried, bullets still had to be metal.) Then, she went and inserted herself in the crowd at the UN in as strategic a location as she could. Muhammad arrived and entered the UN without anything more than shouts, a couple of bottles, and a rock being hurled at him, the last of these being easily deflected by shields in the hands of riot police.

Lacey waited the entire three hours that Muhammad was in the UN. He exited the building and left the grounds, again with nothing more threatening than shouts, bottles, and rocks being hurled. *That's odd*, Lacey thought. She didn't think Pinkies usually missed their marks (and she was right). She guessed that Fred realized the same thing she did: that assassinating Muhammad at the UN would basically be committing suicide (but she was wrong).

Chapter 34
(The Present)

As Lacey was leaving the UN, Chase's rally was starting. One last time, Chase stepped behind his podium in front of his cheering crowd. In a month's time, he had transformed from little more than a snot-nosed nerd into a pillar as strong as an oak tree and, if you asked some people, as big. One last time, Fred's scope-like eye sighted down the barrel of his rifle as his deadly finger caressed his trigger and began to squeeze it ever so slowly and ever so gently. At that very instant, a few hundred yards away, a timer stopped ticking down the seconds and an electrode made contact. An ingeniously engineered hollow sphere of explosives imploded inward toward another sphere of plutonium. The plutonium compressed inward and as it reached its supercritical mass, an uncontrolled cataclysmic chain reaction began. That uncontrolled cataclysmic chain reaction, in turn, detonated a neighboring sphere of fusile material by raising its temperature to that of the core of the sun. Small amounts of the spheres' mass converted to a huge amount of energy, faithfully following Dr. Einstein's famous formula: energy equals mass times the speed of light times the speed of light. Having nowhere to go but out, the huge amount of energy flashed from the spheres, indiscriminately vaporizing everything unlucky enough to be in its way.

Because he was flesh and bones and blood, Chase began vaporizing a tiny fraction of a second before the bullet that had just left Fred's rifle. When the bullet reached its mark, its target was completely gone, as was its shooter. A tiny fraction of a second later, the bullet was completely gone too.

Chapter 35
(The Present)

As Lacey was reaching her hotel, she felt a sharp flash of pain and felt dizzy for a moment. She wasn't sure what it was, but figured it was just part of the mild nausea she'd been feeling the past few days. *I should see a doctor soon*, she thought to herself.

When Lacey got to her room, she was frustrated and exhausted. So, she called room service and ordered some dinner. To save herself the trouble of getting back up, she opened the door to her room and moved the flip-lock over to keep the door slightly ajar. As she sat down, she clicked on the TV. There were images of a blindingly bright flash followed by a rising mushroom cloud. *Great*, she thought, *an uplifting movie to cheer me up*. She started getting worried, though, when every channel she switched to had the same images. "Holy shit," she breathed, "where the hell is this?"

Lacey's worry was replaced by gut-wrenching pain when she realized that what was below the mushroom cloud used to be a large part of Los Angeles. No one on the TV was speaking, but the scrolling text at the bottom of the screen was saying, "... details are sketchy, but ground-zero of the blast seems to have been the UCLA campus ..."

"No!" Lacey screamed. "No, no, no!"

As she sat in stunned trying-not-to-believe silence, room service knocked and Lacey absently said to come in. As the room service server entered the room, she saw Lacey and the state she was in. The room service woman followed Lacey's eyes to the TV and after a few moments, she realized what was going on and she, too, was stunned. Despite what was happening, Lacey glanced at the room service woman for a moment and found her eyes lingering. Behind a cheap pair of glasses and several layers of cheap makeup was a remarkably attractive woman – drop-dead gorgeous some people might say. If Lacey had looked the woman over more carefully, she might have noticed an expensive watch peeking out of the woman's right sleeve that was in stark contrast to her otherwise cheap appearance. But she didn't. The room service woman mumbled something about having a nice dinner or something like that and left. Lacey didn't think about that woman again for several years.

When Lacey was able to gather the little strength she had, she knew there was one thing she had to do. So, she got up to leave. On her way out, she intentionally crashed her dinner to the floor. She had no interest in anything that might sustain her life at that particular moment. She took her laptop to the library and downloaded as much from the Pinky site as she possibly could, which was a lot. She no longer cared if her way into the site was discovered and closed – or about much of anything, for that matter. The Pinkies could go fuck themselves, as far as she was concerned, and everybody else on the planet, too!

Chapter 36
(The Near Future)

As the news spread that much of the population of Los Angeles was completely gone, partially gone, or wishing it was gone, the rest of the world was stunned as though it had been hit hard on the head. People were frozen in place, not able to do the most simple life things, like eat or drink or sleep. People just sat or lay or stood and shook and cried and screamed. And it wasn't only in the United States, either. It was all over the world. And it wasn't because people had deep connections to the late population of Los Angeles, either. In fact, many people in the world who bothered to think about it were pretty sure they didn't even like the late Los Angelenos. They may have even hated them, in fact, because they were pretty sure most of them were overly-affluent, overly-arrogant Americans.

It was because people finally realized that it could have been them who were flesh and bones and blood one second and nothing the next second. More importantly, it could have been their sons and their daughters and their husbands and their wives and their life partners and their mothers and their fathers and their past and present and no-longer future friends. Most importantly, they realized that, except by the grace of God, it could have been them pushing the button that started the timer counting down the seconds, or at least very much wanting to.

Then, the world began to tremble. People began to flutter from place to place, hugging each other and saying how they couldn't believe what had happened and asking if anyone knew anyone who was in L.A. at the time and saying how sorry they were.

Then, the world went into violent convulsions. A few people, in their grief, started breaking windows and then more people joined in. And then everyone joined in, breaking, burning, looting; hitting, hurting, killing. It was as though all of the hate and anger and cruelty of the world got compressed into a supercritical state, leading to an uncontrolled cataclysmic chain reaction with the resulting energy having nowhere else to go but out.

Finally, the convulsions were over. People looked around and saw what they had done and they were sad. They were not just a little on-the-surface sad. They were deeply, agonizingly, gut-wrenchingly sad to see what they had done to the earth and to each other. The world had finally knocked itself hard on its young ass.

Chapter 37
(The Near Future)

The effect of this event, that would later be called the Catalyst event, was that it forced humanity to take stock of itself; as an arrogant, egocentric, narcissistic man might take stock of himself after surviving a failed murder attempt and then turn over a new leaf in his life. The result of humanity taking stock of itself and turning over a new leaf in its life was a step in human evolution somewhat analogous to the step from apes to homo sapiens. But the post-Catalyst step wasn't physical – no spines became straighter and no brains became measurable bigger. Instead, the step was a blend of emotional and intellectual. In a nutshell, people stopped caring deeply about only themselves and their families and started caring deeply about their neighbors – and not just their across the street neighbors, but their around the world neighbors.

This led to a societal maturity that was less egocentric, less selfish, less anxious, and less dog-eat-dog competitive; but was, instead, more humble, more compassionate, and more faithful.

Chapter 38
(The Future)

"That's a remarkable story, Dad," Kurt said sincerely. "One thing, though. How the heck do you know all this?"

"A lot of it I know because, as you know, I've been studying Chase and Lacey for most of my life. But a lot I know from your grandmother."

"Your mother? Grandma Lisa? Did she study Chase and Lacey, too?"

"Come with me for a minute," said Kurt's father. "I want to show you something." Kurt's father led Kurt into his bedroom. Kurt saw immediately that his father's wall safe was open, something he had seen only once before in his life. Kurt also saw a large number of papers and notebooks on his father's bed.

"Are those Grandma Lisa's?" Kurt asked.

"Well, kind of," answered his father. "Here, take a look at this. This is one of your grandmother's journals."

Kurt took the notebook that his father gave him and looked at the name on the inside cover. A chill went down his spine. Not a chill of fear and trepidation, but rather a chill of excitement and exhilaration. "You've got to be kidding me," he said. The name on the inside cover of the journal was *Lacey Howard*. "Grandma *Lisa* was actually Grandma *Lacey*?"

"Yes," his father said.

"So, then who was your father?" Another chill chased the first one back up Kurt's spine and landed in his head, giving it a little tingle. "Wait, don't tell me. Grandpa *Chet* was actually Grandpa *Cha* –"

"Right," Kurt's father interrupted. "My father was Chase Hancock."

"Holy smokes," said Kurt. For one of the few times in his life, he seemed humbled. He started shuffling through the many papers on his father's bed. "Where did all these come from?"

"My mother wrote them, beginning a little before I was born. When she died, I found them."

"How did she die?" Kurt asked.

"She hung herself when I was fifteen years old. I found her in our apartment one afternoon when I got home from school."

"You say that remarkably calmly."

"It was thirty-five years ago, Kurt. I've cried my tears and I'm at peace with it now."

"Why did she kill herself?"

"I don't know."

Kurt found stapled together pages that caught his interest. He started reading through them. "These are the notes for one of Chase's speeches? Wait, I recognize some of these phrases even today. I thought Randal Howard was the main pre-Catalyst intellectual influence. That's what I was taught in school, anyway." A third and final chill went up Kurt's spine. "Randal Howard was my great-grandfather. Wow!"

"Actually, at the end, Chase had as much or more influence as Randy. But that got quickly lost after the Catalyst. Chase was only around a few weeks and wasn't very established. And, needless to say, there was a lot of confusion just after the Catalyst. Chase's words rather quickly got attributed to Randy. "

"Why didn't Lacey set the record straight and why, when we started, did you say that Chase was only a minor figure in the pre-Catalyst?"

"I wasn't sure how far we'd get in the story and it would have been hard to explain without a lot of background. Also, it doesn't really matter whether Chase or Randy gets the credit. Who cares? Lacey didn't and that's one reason she didn't bother setting the record straight. The other bigger reason was that, frankly, she didn't want to draw attention to us. She just wanted to be left alone."

"So, Dad, you know the note that I said I got that had Chase's name on it? It had five words on it all together: 'pinky', 'poison', 'chase', 'hancock', and 'bomb'." Kurt's father went deathly white. Kurt smiled, but not because he had just scared the crap out of his father (well, not entirely because of that, anyway), but because this whole situation was getting very interesting.

Chapter 39
(The Future)

"Do you know who sent you the note?" Kurt's father asked.

"No, I have no idea," Kurt answered.

"What are you going to do if the person tries to contact you again?"

"I have no idea. It'll depend on what the person does next, if anything. The note's probably just someone messing with me."

"I hope so," Kurt's father said. "Whether it's some kind of practical joke or not, please promise me you'll ignore any more attempts at contact."

"I can't promise you that, Dad. Would it be okay if I look this stuff over for a while?" Kurt asked, motioning to the papers on his father's bed.

Kurt's father regarded him for a few moments feeling deeply sad and almost imperceptibly shaking his head from side to side. "I guess so," Kurt's father said. "I guess you're owed at least that. I'll be in the other room."

Handguns were pretty rare in Kurt's time. That's not because handguns were illegal, they weren't. In fact there weren't many things that were illegal in Kurt's time, because laws prohibiting things were far less necessary than they used to be. Handguns were pretty rare because most people didn't feel a need for them anymore. It was partly this rareness that caused the chills that Kurt had experienced a few minutes ago to be replaced by a thrill in the pit of his stomach when he opened a wooden box in his father's safe and found a beautiful fully loaded .38 caliber Smith & Wesson revolver. Nervousness and excitement made Kurt's hand shake as he took the gun out of its velvet lined case and held it.

Kurt didn't act on his first impulse, which was to ask his father where the gun had come from. He expected that it came from Lacey, his grandmother. *Holy shit*, he thought, *maybe it originally came from my great-grandfather's Airborne Ranger weapons stash.*

No, that couldn't be right, he thought. *That would have been in Los Angeles when the Catalyst event happened. Oh well, it was still probably Lacey's.* Kurt took the gun as a sign that reinforced what was already resolving in his mind: he should try to connect with the person who sent him the note. He reached around to his back and slipped the gun under his belt, his hands still shaking. The coolness of the gun felt oddly comforting against his skin. He closed the gun's wooden case and hoped his father wouldn't notice it missing when he put his papers back.

Kurt walked quickly out past his father. "Thanks for everything, Dad," he said as he walked out the front door.

"Wait," his father said, wanting to warn Kurt again to ignore any further attempts at contact from the 'pinky', 'poison', 'chase', 'hancock', and 'bomb' note sender. But it was too late. Kurt was gone. *Typical*, Kurt's father thought, remembering why he liked when his son left.

Chapter 40
(The Future)

The 'pinky', 'poison', 'chase', 'hancock', and 'bomb' note sender didn't leave Kurt much time to ponder whether to ignore further attempts at contact. But, then again, Kurt didn't need much time, because he knew exactly what he was going to do. The morning after Kurt met with his father, the note sender sent Kurt another equally short note: "1023 hamming court, today 1700". Kurt looked up the address and found it to be a currently unused production facility about five miles from his house. At about 4:30 PM, Kurt reached around to his back and again slipped his father's, or probably grandmother's, gun under his belt. Again, his hands were shaking. Again, the coolness of the gun felt oddly comforting against his skin.

Kurt gave Jennifer a quick peck on the cheek and said he had to go out for a while.

"Just a minute," Jennifer said. "I need to tell you something really important."

"It'll have to wait," Kurt said. "I have an appointment." He got into his car and drove to 1023 Hamming Court. As he drove, he got more and more nervous. At the beginning, he thought he could hold himself together. But as he drove, he turned out to be wrong. His hands shook more, his heart raced, sweat soaked his clothes – he was becoming frantic. He could barely keep his car on the road. Part of Kurt's extreme nervousness was because he had a suspicion about who he was about to meet.

When Kurt got to the stated address and got out of his car, the excitement of his adventure overcame his franticness some and he calmed down a bit. When he got to the front door of the building, he gave it a slight push and found it to be unlocked. He pushed it open as quietly as he could and crept in. He pulled his gun out of his belt and cocked the hammer as he had read how to do. He inched into what looked like an empty receptionist's area and didn't see anything other than an open door at the other side of the room. He inched his way to the side of the open door with his gun held in front of him and peaked around through the door. He saw a very large room with nothing in it except what looked like a partial living room setup in a far corner. There was a couch with a coffee table in front of it and with two chairs facing each other at either end of the table. The couch and chairs were comfortable looking, as far as he could tell from his distance, and there was a picture of what looked like old Los Angeles on the wall behind the couch. A person was in one of the chairs with his or her back to him, it was hard to tell which.

Just then, Jennifer tried to net Kurt. *Jesus Christ, not now!* he thought to himself, and ignored the net.

Kurt raised his gun up in front of him again and slowly moved in through the door and across the floor.

With each step, his nervousness increased, as it had in his car. As he got closer to the chairs, he could see that the person sitting in one of them was a woman. When he got within about 20 feet, she stood up slowly, turned around, and said, "Hello, Kurt, my dear."

By this time, Kurt's nervousness had reached franticness again. With his gun trembling in his grip, he screamed at the woman, "Show me your left hand and bend only your God damned fucking pinky!"

The woman lifted her hand and bent her pinky with no trouble. Kurt breathed a sigh of relief, but it was short lived. He noticed an expensive watch peeking out of the woman's right sleeve and an uncomfortable thought crossed his mind. "Now, show me your right hand," he said.

The woman raised her right hand.

"Bend only your pinky," Kurt said fiercely.

After a brief hesitation, the woman slowly lowered her hand and said, "I can't."

"Oh my God... Lena!" Kurt said. He wobbled a little bit and then mumbled more to himself than to her: "Left-handed Lena."

"Why did you want to see me?" Kurt asked, gaining back a bit of his composure.

David W. Palmer

"I thought you might want to know a few things, and then I have a bit of business to conduct with you," she answered.

"Wait, if you're really Lena, there's no way I could have just snuck up on you with a gun in my hand. What's this really all about? Why this little masquerade?" Kurt asked.

"I've spent the last fifty-five years of my life protecting my identity," she responded. "Setting up this little situation where you could 'discover' who I was just made it a little easier for me. Now, why don't you put the gun down... I think we're going to be here a while." She was right.

If he were to think back on it, Kurt wouldn't have really known why he did it. It's like he trusted her a little bit, or he knew it was the right thing to do, or something like that. He put his gun down.

Chapter 41
(The Future)

As Kurt sat down across from Lena, she said to him, "So, I know your father told you who your grandparents were."

"How do you know that?" Kurt asked.

"I have my ways," Lena answered. "I also know he told you who your great grandfather was. But he didn't tell you the whole story."

"What do you mean he didn't tell me the whole story?"

"He didn't tell you what your great grandfather did before he became your great grandfather."

"He most certainly did," Kurt said, starting to get defensive. "He was an Airborne Ranger in Vietnam. He even lost his hand near the end of the war."

"No, that's not right. That's what your father thinks. But that's not right."

"Oh, really?" Kurt said. "What's right, then?"

"Give me a few minutes to get to that. I don't want to get too far ahead of myself."

"Yeah, I wouldn't want you to get too far ahead of yourself," Kurt said with more than a hint of sarcasm in his voice.

"Well, you are your grandmother's grandson. That's for sure," Lena said.

That comment jolted Kurt. It brought home to him that he was sitting with a contemporary of Chase and Lacey, a person who knew them (or at least knew Lacey), a person who he could learn a lot from. He toned himself down a bit. "Okay, sorry," he said. "Go ahead. I want to hear your story."

Chapter 42
(The Near Future)

As was mentioned earlier, several years passed between when Lacey saw the room service woman in her hotel by the United Nations and when she thought about her again. During that time, a lot happened in Lacey's life. As the world finished freezing in shock, trembling, and convulsing in reaction to the Catalyst event, what she had begun suspecting was confirmed – she was pregnant. This, combined with everything else that was happening, threw her into a deep depression. Even for a person as strong as Lacey, this was understandable. After all, the world seemed to be crumbling around her and everything that was familiar to her, everything that she depended on, everything that supported her was gone: her father, her boyfriend, her home, her university, her car. Even most of the money she would have inherited from her father was still in probate and was now less than vapor, along with nearly everything else of hers.

There were two exceptions to this. One was a few tens of thousands of dollars that had been put into a trust fund for her when her mother died and was now in a bank that mirrored its account data in several sites around the country. The other was the thing that made her life nearly unbearable in the short term but finally saved her life in the longer term – the baby she was expecting. How the hell could she support a baby? She couldn't even support herself. Several times she thought that she could save both herself and her expected baby a huge amount of trouble by ending both of their lives. Several other times she thought that she could save both herself and her expected baby a huge amount of trouble by ending only her expected baby's life. After all, if she killed herself, her expected baby would die anyway, right? And what baby would want to be brought into the world as it was now, anyway, right? Right? She went so far as to visit an abortion clinic and found something she didn't expect: a line of women stretching nearly around the block, as though they were waiting to get into the latest blockbuster horror film. Apparently she wasn't the only post-Catalyst woman planning to save herself and her expected baby a huge amount of trouble.

As Lacey waited in the line of women stretching nearly around the block, she had a realization. What she was about to kill was her only connection back to the people she loved, back to Chase, back to her father. Did she really want to lose her father, her boyfriend, her home, her university, her car, *and* her expected baby? *What the fuck am I doing?* she thought to herself. "I can't do this," she said out loud. She stepped out of line and started to walk away.

"You go, girl," the woman who had been behind Lacey in line said softly. Lacey didn't hear her. A tear rolled down the woman's cheek as she let the gap that Lacey had left in the line linger for a few moments. *I can't do this, either*, the woman thought to herself as she took a small step toward following Lacey. "Wait, what the fuck am I doing?" she said out loud. She stepped back in line and filled in Lacey's gap. Another tear rolled down the woman's cheek. But she stayed in the line of women stretching nearly around the block anyway.

With Lacey's realization came a reason for living, a purpose. With that, she snapped herself out of her depression and resolved to scrape together a little life for herself and her expected baby, despite the Catalyst event. She further resolved to scrape out a little happiness to go along with the little life, if there was any of that left to be had. There was, in fact, some of that left to be had – for a few years anyway.

The first thing Lacey did was withdraw her few tens of thousands of dollars from the bank that mirrored its account data in several sites around the country. She then went to the city hall and changed her name. The clerk resisted at first, because Lacey wasn't a resident of New York. Lacey pointed out that a lot of the city that she *was* a resident of wasn't there anymore. Lacey explained that she wanted to change her name to distance herself from her previous life (which was true, but for considerably more complicated reasons than she cared to explain to the clerk). The clerk saw her point, took pity on her, and changed her name to what she requested: Lacey Phoenix. Yeah, she knew that was corny. But what the hell.

Lacey found a small apartment in the upper west side of Manhattan, not too far from the George Washington Bridge, where she lived on her few tens of thousands dollars as she awaited her expected baby. Not being one to just sit on her continually-widening ass, she took on several activities. She joined a gym near her apartment and did aerobic workouts several times a week, starting with classes for everyone and then moving into classes for expectant moms. She took a class for new mothers to learn how to feed her baby, how to change diapers, and how to do the many other things that go along with caring for a baby – things that were pretty much the farthest thing from her mind just a short number of months before.

Lacey spent time poring over all the data she had downloaded from the Pinky site the day of the Catalyst event. She learned several things, like the instructed mode of a Pinky killing was almost always *Covert* and almost never *Assassination*. This surprised her a little because most of the instructions she had seen before were for assassinations – although, two of those were for Chase, now that she thought about it. The data soon became rather boring partly because the thousands of files, with nothing but cryptic codes and dates in their filenames, were cumbersome to get through and partly because the files were mainly instructions and follow-up reports.

Lacey was amazed by some of the names in the instructions – some famous, some becoming famous, and some only potentially famous. She did some Internet searches on some of the potentially famous people and found them to be an impressive bunch. In sum, it was amazing to her how many influential people, or potentially influential people, were cut down by car crashes, drug overdoses, freak accidents, induced illnesses, mock assassinations, or what have you. *These people made the mistake of being influential outside the narrow bounds prescribed by the establishment,* she thought to herself, *or at least the PCA's interpretation of those bounds.*

After Lacey had some morbid amusement with the names, there didn't seem to be much more of interest. She had a fleeting thought of turning the data into the authorities. But then she realized that, in a real sense, the Pinkies were the authorities and trying to turn them in, so to speak, would have little more effect than buying herself a one-way ticket to the morgue.

Lacey took a bus down to Columbia University twice a week and audited a course in advanced mathematics, her major at Caltech. This was particularly fortunate for her, because the professor of the course was impressed with her math skills and her assertive personality and developed an interest in her. Toward the end of the term (both the course's and hers), the professor told her about a long-term substitute teaching position opening up in about four months at George Washington High School, not too far from her apartment. Appropriately enough, the position was opening up because a teacher was going out on maternity leave. Lacey had told the professor before that, although she had finished most of her course work at Caltech, she hadn't actually walked across the stage to receive her diploma. So, she hadn't actually graduated. Even though she knew it would probably cost her a job that she desperately needed, she reminded the professor of that fact.

That didn't matter, the professor said. She clearly had a strong grasp of her subject and the personality to deal with a bunch of unruly teenagers. Besides, although Caltech was far enough away from ground zero of the Catalyst event to still be standing, it was close enough to be evacuated due to high levels of radiation. So, there was nobody there with whom to check her credentials. Even if there was, huge numbers of electronic records were destroyed by the Catalyst blast's electromagnetic pulse, most certainly including Caltech's. The professor asked Lacey what her GPA was, speaking of records. 4.0, she answered. That's what he figured. He said that the little white lie that she had graduated when she actually hadn't would be forgiven in the overall scheme of things. He also said that he knew the principal at George Washington High School and that he would be happy to recommend her.

Lacey was a little worried that the professor might want a little something in return for his spirited support of her. But it turned out he didn't. He was just a nice person. And he was right, Lacey made an excellent teacher. Her long-term sub position turned into a permanent position that she stayed in until her end.

Chapter 43
(The Near Future)

When Lacey's time came, she delivered a beautiful baby boy at the New York Presbyterian hospital. She named him Hosea, which means salvation. Lacey took Hosea home and they lived frugal but reasonably happy lives for several years.

During those years, Lacey was conflicted by a need to stay under the radar, for Hosea's sake as much as anything, and a growing feeling of responsibility to stand up and do what she could to help the world and her fellow humans. She ended up doing her best to do both. She anonymously released Chase's speech notes and part of the story behind them and watched as they were woven into the world's psyche. She watched Chase's words get misattributed to her father as time went by, but she didn't really care. She also helped the world and her fellow humans in small ways, as best she could, like giving what little she could to feed the hungry and other such things. After the Catalyst, a lot more people seemed to be doing a lot more of that and it was having a remarkably positive effect.

During those years, Lacey had two startling revelations; the first one close to fatal, the second completely fatal. The first one came when she was poking around in her Pinky data as she still did every now and then. She had started looking at location files lately. Each Pinky must have had tracking devices built in, because there was a file for every hour of every day containing the initial of each Pinky followed by a position given in latitude and longitude. It was the latitude and longitude part that had kept her from spending much time with the location files before, because it was inconvenient mapping them to geographic locations. But she had been doing it lately anyway pretty much for fun, to see just how much the Pinkies got around. It turned out that, as she expected, Pinkies got around a lot – all over the country and (slightly surprisingly) all over the world.

But then she noticed two things: one kind of curious and the other very curious. The kind of curious thing was that the Pinky with initial 'P', Primo, dropped off the location files. This was only kind of curious because she had noticed long ago that Primo's instructions and follow-up reports had stopped. The very curious thing was that the Pinky with initial 'R', Ringo, didn't drop off the location files, even though his instructions and follow-up reports had stopped. Instead, Ringo's location just became much more stable. The only thing she could conclude was that Primo had died and Ringo hadn't. For fun, she found Ringo's most common nighttime coordinates and his most common daytime coordinates and mapped them onto geographic locations. When she was done, Lacey breathed words she hadn't used in many years – "Holy fucking shit." The daytime location was her father's building on the UCLA campus and the nighttime location was her home in L.A. "This can't be," she said out loud.

To check further, Lacey looked at some of the location files around the time of her father's death. Sure enough, the 'R' entries stopped the day of his death, with a notation on the last entry that said, 'deceased'. Previous to that, there were notations in the entries that said, 'ill-9.3', 'ill-8.9', that kind of thing. Some Pinkies must have had built-in health monitors to go along with their built-in tracking devices.

Needless to say, it was difficult for Lacey to process this revelation. At an intellectual level, it explained a lot, she thought. It explained her father's personality when she was young. It explained why her father freaked out when her mother died. *Hmm*, she thought to herself, *I wonder if my mother's death was a Pinky killing. I'll have to check one day – although, I'm not sure I really want to know, at this point.* It explained why her father gave her four years of Airborne Ranger training – wait, check that, four years of Pinky training. *Holy fucking shit...* It explained her father's continually being tormented by demons. It explained his intense need to *fix* the world. It probably even explained why he ended up in the hospital he did, rather than the UCLA Medical Center – the PCA must have had a doctor or two on the payroll at that hospital. Her father had some hardware installed that would be hard to explain to inquiring doctors at the Medical Center.

There was one big question this revelation raised for Lacey, though. If the PCA knew where her father, Ringo, was, as they obviously did, why did they let him be? Maybe, ironically, the PCA leadership actually had a heart. Maybe, as long has Ringo behaved himself, they were willing to let him live a normal life. Maybe it wasn't until he started being influential outside the narrow bounds prescribed by the establishment that that had to change.

Lacey had all these intellectual thoughts over a course of about a minute. But then the emotional implications started setting in: her father, the man who raised her, the man she trusted over all other people, the man she loved as only a child can love a parent, was one of the most cunning, creative, ruthless killers on the planet, ever. She tried to review her Pinky research in her mind, remembering the hundreds of people Ringo had killed, most of them mostly innocent.

This revelation threw Lacey back into a depression similar to the one she was in right after the Catalyst and for a similar reason – her world had been ripped out from under her feet. Although she hid it reasonably well from Hosea and her students, she suffered the depression for many days. More than once she contemplated putting herself out of her misery. Finally, she went so far as to find a length of rope in her junk closet and look for a place to hang it. There was a large hook in the corner of her bedroom on which someone had obviously hung a heavy plant. *That couldn't possibly support my weight*, she thought. She put her desk chair in the corner, looped the rope through the hook, grabbed the rope with both hands, and kicked the chair out of the way. She was wrong, the hook held her weight.

Lacey put a head-sized loop in the rope and tied the other end to the hook. She then went back into her junk closet and found a package of large plastic tie wraps that Hosea had needed for a school project. One end of each of the tie wraps had a little slot that Lacey could push the other end through as far as she wanted to. Once pushed in, it would be nearly impossible to pull the end back out again. Lacey was going to use one of these to bind her hands behind her back. Lacey stood back up on the chair, put her head through the loop in her rope, and tightened it.

Two more steps, Lacey thought to herself as she stood on her chair with the tie wrap in her hand, *bind my hands and kick the chair*.

Do I really want to do this? she asked herself for the final time. *What about Hosea? What about my students? My father did many, many terrible things. He was a very bad man. But that was a long time ago. And he changed. He became a good man. He ended up doing many good things. My father paid for his sins. Why should I? Why should Hosea? I don't know. But I'm not sure I can live with what I now know...* She put her hands behind her back and started slowly slipping the free end of her tie wrap into the other end.

A few moments later, Hosea got home and said, "Mom, I'm home. Where are you?" He knocked on his mother's bedroom door and then went in.

"I'm right here, honey," Lacey said, pushing her desk chair back under her desk.

Hosea noticed some tear streaks on his mother's face. "What are you doing, Mom?" he asked. "Are you okay?"

"I was just thinking about some things, honey," Lacey answered. "Yes, I'm okay." And she was.

Chapter 44
(The Near Future)

Lacey's second revelation came with a knock on the door. Lacey was home sick for one of the few times in her life and wasn't expecting anyone. When she answered the door, Lacey saw an oddly familiar face. Although many years had gone by and the cheap pair of glasses and the several layers of cheap makeup were gone, Lacey recognized the woman at her door as the remarkably attractive room service woman from her hotel by the United Nations. "Can I help you?" Lacey asked falteringly.

"You recognize me, don't you?" the woman asked.

"Yes, you brought me room service at a hotel I stayed in about fifteen years ago."

"Yes, that's right. I meant to kill you that night."

"Excuse me?" Lacey said.

"I said I meant to kill you that night," the woman answered. "My name is Thumbelina. As you know, my acquaintances call me Lena."

Lacey stood in silence for several moments. "Please forgive me," she said. "I must admit I was never expecting to meet you and even if I was, I never would have expected you to be quite so forthright. Can I assume that, since you're here talking to me instead of shooting me or poisoning me or sabotaging my car, you're not here to kill me?"

"Not right at the moment, anyway," Lena said with a slight smile.

"How comforting," Lacey said. "So, what do you want?"

"I know you've made a bit of a hobby out of Pinky history. There are at least a couple of things I doubt you've figured out and that you might be interested in."

"I know my father was Ringo, if that's what you want to tell me. I figured that out about five years ago."

"Smart girl," Lena said slightly condescendingly. "But I know you know your father was Ringo."

"And just how do you know that?"

"You're not the only one with hobbies, you know."

"So, I'm, like, your hobby?"

"Can I come in?" Lena asked.

"I'm pretty sure I'm going to regret this. But, yeah, okay." Lacey let Lena in, led her into her sparse living room, and offered her a seat in a worn but otherwise comfortable flower-patterned armchair. "Can I offer you something to drink?"

"I would kill for some coffee," Lena said. Seeing Lacey's expression, she quickly added, "Sorry, just a little Pinky humor. How about a cup of coffee?"

"Sure," Lacey said. As she went into the kitchen, she thought to herself that, under different circumstances, she would probably like Lena. She came back into the living room with two cups of coffee.

With the pleasantries out of the way, Lacey asked her question again, "So, I'm, like, your hobby?"

"Well, kind of," Lena answered. "I have been keeping a bit of an eye on you, and ear, for that matter." Lacey saw her glance up at the ceiling light fixture.

"There's a bug up there, isn't there?"

"Like I said, smart girl."

"But why?" Lacey asked.

"Why what?"

"Why am I kind of one of your hobbies?" Lacey was getting a little impatient.

"A few reasons, really. One is that you were a first for me. You were the first kill that I didn't follow through on – the only one, for that matter."

"How were you going to do it?"

"Do what?"

"Kill me. How the hell were you going to kill me?"

"The dinner that you dumped on the floor at the hotel had the same poison in it that Dex used on your father, except a hair more to make sure you wouldn't suffer for long."

"Gee, thanks. How thoughtful of you. Like father like daughter, was that the idea?"

"Pretty much. Maybe genetic, maybe environmental, maybe you were both drunks. It's doubtful the coroner would have worried about it long enough to detect the poison, especially since the poison is very hard to detect, anyway."

"So, why didn't you finish?"

"Finish what?

"Me, God damn it, why didn't you finish killing me? Are you always this hard to talk to?"

"Well, I haven't had a huge amount of practice, really. You're not exactly the easiest person to talk to right now, either, you know."

"Yes, you're right. Sorry. I guess I'm a bit nervous. I'll try harder. So, why didn't you finish killing me?"

"Well, I didn't want to kill you to begin with. I usually have absolutely no feeling about my targets. But you were different. As you can imagine, Pinkies don't have much of a life. When your father dropped off the grid and they let him get away with it, I started living vicariously through him, just a little bit – I think we all did. That might be partly why they let him get away with it, I'm not sure – for the sanity of the rest of us. Then, when you were born, well, it's like I had a niece."

"You knew about me?"

"Yes, I knew about you and I cared about you and I kept an eye on you when I could. Your father didn't know it, but I watched you grow up from a baby."

"Wait, I thought Pinkies didn't know who other Pinkies were."

"That's part of the Pinky legend, partly because it was true for the first several years. As time went by, though, we became acquainted with each other one way or another. It's not like we had office parties or anything. But we knew each other and even liked each other to the degree that we could. Dex was pretty upset when he found out he had to take out your father. That might be why he partially botched the kill, I don't know.

"So, anyway, I cared about you. I also admired you. You had developed into a very capable young woman. The way you took out Dex was outstanding. You are either very skilled or very lucky. Actually, you're probably a bit of both. But that's true for all of us, really. In any case, none of us could have done better."

"So, they knew I took out Dex?"

"Of course they knew, sweetie. That's one of the reasons I was supposed to take you out to begin with. The other was that you were supporting that shit-disturber, Chase Hancock."

"Be careful, you're talking about the only man I've ever loved and the father of my child."

"I know. But he was still a shit-disturber, at least in the eyes of my bosses."

"Are there any other reasons? Wait, let me be clearer. Are there any other reasons why you didn't finish killing me?"

"The other reason is that that's about the only time I actually could get away without finishing you. As you know, the Catalyst event threw pretty much everything into huge turmoil. Little problems like you got lost in the noise. Not to mention that, for obvious reasons, Chase Hancock was no longer a problem. Sorry, I'm being insensitive. See, not a lot of practice.

"By the time the dust settled, so to speak, and people got back to worrying about little problems like you, you had settled yourself and you weren't such a problem anymore. That's another reason you're kind of one of my hobbies, though, by the way."

"To make sure I keep my nose clean? Is that really necessary anymore? I mean, in case your bosses haven't noticed, the world has been changing quite a bit lately."

"Yeah, they realize they're getting a bit obsolete. But, oh well..."

"Monitoring people isn't a normal Pinky activity, is it?"

"No, you're special, sweetie."

"Please don't call me sweetie, okay?"

"Okay, I'll try."

Chapter 45
(The Near Future)

"So, if you didn't want to tell me that my father was Ringo, what did you want to tell me?" Lacey asked.

"I'll get to that," Lena responded. "But we'll probably never talk to each other again. So, is there anything that's been nagging you? Are there any gaps I can fill in for you?"

"Well, now that you mention it, I have been wondering why my father left the Pinkies to begin with."

"Oh, you haven't figured that little tidbit out yet? You know your father was the one who had to kill Primo, right?"

"No, I actually hadn't come across that yet," Lacey answered. Not many things startled her these days. But this did – she wasn't expecting it.

"That was all before my time. I wasn't even born yet, actually. But, from what I've heard, killing Primo really freaked Ringo out. In our training, it was drilled into us that we are invincible. That's an attitude you kind of have to have to be a Pinky. But, if Ringo could take Primo out, what was to keep the next Pinky on the list from taking him out? This forced look at his mortality made Ringo start thinking about other things, too. Like was being one of the most cunning, creative, ruthless killers on the planet, ever, what he really wanted to do with his life?

"To his credit, Ringo hung in with the program for quite a while. But then, after about five years, he couldn't take it any more. To sever himself from the Pinky program, both figuratively and literally, he took a hatchet and chopped off his left hand. I think you know the rest."

Lacey was silent for what seemed like several minutes. "So, the whole Vietnam thing was complete bullshit?"

"I'm afraid so, sweetie. Oh, sorry."

"Even after I knew my dad was Ringo, I still clung to the Vietnam part of the story. You know, after he left the Pinkies. I'm not sure why I did that. I guess it was kind of redeeming. If I'd bothered figuring out his timeline more carefully, I would have realized that Vietnam wouldn't have been possible. Oh well..." Lacey sounded dejected. "So, I guess since you didn't know I didn't know that, that's not what you came to tell me."

"No. But you seem pretty down. Maybe I shouldn't tell you any more."

"No, that's okay," said Lacey. "I doubt if it can get much worse."

"Okay, if you say so. It would help to look at some Pinky files for this, okay?"

"Sure, why not. My computer's in my bedroom. Sorry, it's kind of messy in there. I'm sick."

"It's okay. It's nothing I haven't seen before."

Lacey gave Lena a sideways glance. "Do you mean *my* messy bedroom or messy bedrooms, in general? Oh, never mind. I probably don't really want to know." Lacey picked up a kitchen chair and led Lena into her bedroom.

"Here... Here's an updated set of data," said Lena, taking a thumb drive out of her pocket and handing it to Lacey.

"Where did you get this? Are you supposed to have this?" asked Lacey as she plugged in the little drive.

"Let's just say I've taken up your interest in Pinky history."

Lena handed Lacey a list of files. "Start with the first file on the list." Lacey opened the file. It looked like a typical Pinky location file. "That's the Catalyst device blast location, calculated by experts with an accuracy of a few square feet. It was a parking garage on the UCLA campus."

"That's interesting," said Lacey. "So what?"

"Now, open the next file. That's the Pinky location file for fourteen weeks before the Catalyst event, the day your father fell ill. Notice the location of initial 'R', Ringo."

"So, my father was in a parking garage at UCLA. That's where he worked. So, big deal."

"He was there for three hours. He was also in the exact same location for at least a couple of hours a few days before."

"So what? My father must have been discussing politics with a colleague, or tutoring a student who didn't want to be seen being tutored, or having a bloody affair, or whatever. Who knows? Who cares at this point?"

"The next file, go ahead open it, shows one-way plane tickets for your father and you for two days after he fell ill. Did you know about those? Did you also know that he transferred a large sum of money to an overseas account a few days previous to that?"

"No, I didn't know that. But so what! My father was going to surprise me with a vacation or something!

It was around Christmas time, right? I see where you're going with this, by the way, and you are dead wrong!"

"The next file shows your father's location a few weeks earlier – in the same proximity as three Russian physicists who were suspected of having a pirated Soviet nuclear bomb in their possession. The location was raided shortly thereafter. The device was not found. But there was evidence that it had been there. All three of those physicists wound up dead a few days later. Your father's locations match the locations of their 'accidents'."

"My father did go on a couple of trips around that time. But those were business. That's what my father said and he didn't lie!"

"Sweetie, remember who we're talking about, here."

"We're talking about my God damned father. That's who we're talking about! If this was all going on, why didn't somebody stop it at the time?"

"These connections were all put together after the fact. If anyone had put them together at the time, it would have been stopped. I'm sorry."

Tears were streaming down Lacey's face. "This cannot be! This is all circumstantial. Is this all you have?"

"No, I'm sorry, sweetie, I have one more thing. What five words did your father say to you when he gained semi-consciousness in the hospital?"

"He said 'pinky', 'poison', 'chase', 'hancock', and... 'bomb'." Lacey burst into tears. "Why the hell are you telling me this?"

"I just thought you'd want to know, sweetie." Lena leaned sideways to try to hug Lacey.

"Don't," Lacey screamed, pushing Lena away. "Get out of here! Get out! Now!"

"Okay," said Lena, "I'm going." As she got up, she leaned over and kissed Lacey on the cheek. "I love you, sweetie," she said. And she left.

Chapter 46
(The Near Future)

Lacey didn't do any intellectual or emotional processing with this revelation. The guilt of knowing her father had set the Catalyst bomb, on top of everything else she had dealt with over the past years, was simply more than she could take. Instead of thinking or feeling anything other than numbness, she moved her desk chair into the corner of her bedroom and dug the rope and the tie wrap out of the drawer she had thrown them into about five years before. She stood up on her chair, tied the rope to the large hook, put her head through the loop in the other end, and tightened it. She put her hands behind her back, slipped the free end of her tie wrap into the other end, and pulled it tight. She kicked the chair.

At that instant, her body's basic instinct to stay alive took over. She struggled desperately to free her hands. But she couldn't. She kicked and gyrated wildly to try to get the rope off the hook. But she couldn't. She struggled desperately to breathe. But she couldn't. As her body gave up its futile struggle, she found that her life did, in fact, flash before her eyes just as people said it would.

She remembered her mother's wavy dark hair with a faint vanilla scent, her dark almond eyes, and being held by her. She remembered her father's intense caring for her. She remembered meeting Chase in the library and loving him and being loved by him. She remembered the positive effect that her father and Chase and she had on the world. She remembered having Hosea and loving him as only a parent can love a child. She remembered her students and the fun she had with them and the constructive impact she had on their lives. She remembered meeting Lena and knowing that she could have liked her. And, then, she didn't remember any more.

Instead, she saw space compressed into an infinitesimally small spinning point. She saw the point explode with an intensely blinding flash of energy. She saw the still spinning violently expanding energy cloud start to coalesce into subatomic particles and then into atoms. She saw the still growing cloud of energy and atoms begin to break up into huge spinning balls that started to flatten into disks. She saw the spinning disks start to break up further to form stars. She saw the stars form and explode over and over again, eventually also forming planets in the cycles. She saw civilizations rise and fall in the blink of an eye. She saw that eventually there was nothing more to explode and there was instead an immeasurably large ball of spinning energy that would normally begin contracting. At this point for Lacey, though, the spinning ball of energy dissolved into nothingness. Then, she felt as one with all that ever was, all that is, and all that will ever be and she was at peace.

As Lacey walked through the door to eternity, her son, Hosea, walked through the door of their apartment. "Hi, Mom, I'm home," he said. "Where are you? Are you feeling better?" He knocked on his mother's bedroom door and then went in...

Chapter 47
(The Near Future)

If Lacey could have gotten into the Pinky site, she would have found that this instruction had been sent to Lena's intracranial receiver:

> *TARGET: Lacey Anita Phoenix, math teacher,*
> *George Washington High School, New York*
> *City; PRIORITY: Medium; MODE: Covert.*
> *– REPEAT –*
> *TARGET: Lacey Anita Phoenix, math teacher,*
> *George Washington High School, New York*
> *City; PRIORITY: Medium; MODE: Covert.*

But Lacey couldn't get into the Pinky site because her way in had been blocked many years ago and, well, because she was dead.

Chapter 48
(The Future)

"I'm not sure why I got that instruction," Lena said to Kurt. "I know the PCA was on its last legs and maybe somebody was in cleanup mode or something like that. What I do know is it was the last instruction I ever got."

Kurt was barely listening at that point. He had a slight smile on his lips. "Wait," he interrupted, "let me get this straight. My great-grandfather was the Pinky called Ringo. And he was Randal Howard, the man who dared to challenge the establishment even though he knew the other Pinkies were out there. And he was Fidele Veritas, the man who set the Catalyst bomb. My grandmother was Lacey Howard, the woman who single-handedly took out Dex and empowered Chase Hancock. My grandfather was Chase Hancock, another man who dared to challenge the establishment knowing what had happened to Randal Howard and who significantly influenced society, even today, albeit anonymously! I seem to come from a long line of very dangerous people."

"Yes, you do, dear," Lena said. She wanted to follow up with, "*And you're doing your best to keep that tradition going, aren't you?*" But she didn't.

"It's amazing my father turned out as normally as he did."

"Oh, he had his moments, believe me; particularly after he found his mother. But that's a whole other story."

Kurt was receiving another net from Jennifer, but he ignored it. "I kind of interrupted you, there," he said to Lena. "What were you saying?"

"I was saying, I'm not sure why I got the instruction to take out Lacey. More importantly, I'm not sure why I carried the instruction out. I struggled with it. But in the end my many years of training, experience, and professional pride won out, I guess. I was being instructed to clean up the only blotch on my otherwise spotless record. It didn't matter in the end, I guess, that I had become fond of that blotch.

"I was also saying that the instruction to take out Lacey was the last one I ever got. It took me about six months to realize that for sure. Instructions came erratically. They didn't come on any schedule or anything. But the longest gap I could remember before Lacey was about three months. So, in the fourth month, I started to wonder. In the fifth month, I called my handler's phone number for the first time ever to try to find out what was going on. As I pretty much expected, there was no answer. In the sixth month, my monthly salary didn't get put into my account. That pretty much clinched it for me. Even so, as much out of curiosity as anything, I went to the Pinky headquarters to see what I could see. I had been there once before, so I knew where it was."

"When were you there before?" Kurt asked.

Chapter 49
(The Past)

Susan was pretty nervous as the man she was riding with, Mr. White, parked the car. Susan had been on the streets for a few years by then and had seen quite a bit. But she had never seen a building quite like the one she and Mr. White were now parking across the street from. The building itself wasn't that unusual. It was a pretty plain looking six story office building, in fact – pretty big as far as six story office buildings go; but otherwise pretty plain. What made the building unusual was that chain link fence with looped razor wire surrounded the whole building except a gate at the front. Not only one chain link fence with looped razor wire, but two chain link fences with looped razor wire, one inside the other, with about ten yards of no-man's land in between. The gate at the front was guarded by four people in army uniforms carrying government issued M-16 rifles. Other people, also in army uniforms and carrying government issued M-16 rifles, were patrolling the fences.

Susan had never been to the Washington DC suburb she was in now. So, for all she knew, the building she was staring at could have been completely common. The building wasn't that common, in fact. But there were enough like it sprinkled around that anyone who had been in the area for a while would likely not have given it a second look.

"Ready, Susan?" Mr. White asked, looking at her staring at the building.

"Yeah, I guess so," Susan answered. They got out of the car and walked into a building next to where they had parked, across the street from the building with the chain link fence, razor wire, and M-16s. There they got Susan a visitor's badge and then walked across the street. Even though the guard that Mr. White approached clearly recognized him, he checked his badge anyway. The same guard scrutinized Susan and her visitor's badge and eventually let her pass. As Susan and Mr. White approached the building, she noticed that the lawn and shrubbery behind the fence were immaculately kept and that even the building was very clean. As they walked in the front door, Susan was met by a drab green but nevertheless clean and orderly lobby, with hallways leading off from that lobby in three directions. Susan and Mr. White entered an elevator and he pressed the button for the sixth floor.

"The agency we're visiting occupies the top three floors of the building," Mr. White said as they were going up. "Another three-letter agency occupies the bottom three floors and serves as a cover for the one we're visiting."

"Should you really be telling me that?" Susan asked.

"Sure, why not? One way or another, you won't be in a position to spread that little tidbit around." That sounded a bit ominous and didn't help Susan's nerves.

When they got off the elevator, Mr. White led Susan to an office in the corner of the building. There was a secretary's desk in a cubicle outside the door, but nobody was at the desk. Mr. White knocked on the door.

"Come in," someone inside said. As Susan and Mr. White entered the large office, she saw a little gray haired man behind a large ornate desk that seemed at least two sizes too big for him. The man had a grey beard to match his hair and he was wearing a gray tweed sport jacket with the brown elbow patches that had been in style years ago, but weren't any more. The man got up, walked around his desk, and slowly looked Susan up and down. "She's very pretty," he said to Mr. White.

"Yes she is, sir," Mr. White said.

"Tell me where you found her, again," the man said to Mr. White, as though Susan wasn't even there.

"I found her in San Francisco, sir."

"How old is she?"

"She's fifteen, sir."

"And how long has she been on the streets?"

"Three years, sir."

"And she did well on the tests?"

"The best yet, sir."

"Outstanding. What's your name, dear?" the man said addressing Susan for the first time.

"Susan Smith, sir."

"Come on, what's your *real* name, dear?"

"It's really Susan Smith, sir," she answered. The man glanced over at Mr. White who nodded almost imperceptibly.

"'Smith' – outstanding. Why did you come here, Susan Smith?"

"Mr. White has been convincing me that I can help the world by working for you, sir. He said I'm particularly suited for the work that you need done, sir."

"Good. So, why did you leave home, Susan?"

"My father used to get drunk off his ass and beat the shit out of mother, sir."

"My, my... such language for a young woman. So, you couldn't take your father beating up your mother anymore and so you left?"

"Not exactly, sir. My father died when I was twelve. The coroner said he must have eaten some rat poison. His death was ruled a suicide. But a lot of people thought my mother probably poisoned him."

"Your mother didn't poison your father, did she, dear?"

"No, she didn't, sir."

"So, with your father out of the way, why did you leave home?"

"My mother said she never wanted to see me again, sir."

"Have you ever seen anyone die, Susan?"

"No, sir. Not really, sir. I heard someone get shot in an abandoned building I was crashing in. But it was dark and I couldn't really see much. So, no, sir."

"Come with me," the little man said. Susan and Mr. White followed him into a projection room with a large screen. "Sit down here, Susan, in the front row. What you are about to see is real. It is not actors making believe. The man you will see had a wife who loved him and a daughter just a little younger than you who also loved him." The little man motioned to a window at the back of the room and a movie started.

The movie showed a man tied to a chair whose face had been savagely beaten. He was pleading with the two men standing by him to stop; he would do whatever they wanted. Instead of stopping, one of the men punched him hard in the face. The crunching sound and the blood that poured from the deep new cut under the man's left eye were sickening. The other man grabbed the bound man's hair from behind, yanked his head back, and sliced his throat. Blood spurted profusely and Susan could see the man's windpipe from the inside. She fell forward onto her hands and knees and vomited violently.

"She'll do," the little man said, with Susan still on all fours. "From this moment onward, her name is Thumbelina."

"Thumbelina... that's very clever, sir."

"Thank you," the little man said with a wry little smile. "You can go now. And I never want to see her here again."

"Yes, sir. Thank you, sir," said Mr. White. He went and helped Thumbelina to her feet and the two of them left.

Chapter 50
(The Future)

"So, anyway," Lena continued, "in the sixth month, when I went to the Pinky headquarters to see what I could see, it looked pretty decrepit. The once immaculately kept lawns and shrubs were then weeds and out-of-control bushes. The once very clean building was then dirty, stained, and old looking. There was a single guard at the gate sitting in a chair with his government issued M-16 leaning against his little guard house. It looked like he was there more to keep curious sightseers out than anything else at that point. As I drove slowly by, I couldn't help but think that the guard bore an uncanny resemblance to Dr. Brown, the little gray haired mastermind of the Pinky program with the too-big desk and the out-of-style sport jacket. But it couldn't have been him. He would have been in his late eighties or early nineties by then.

"It turned out to be good for me that the Pinky program chose that time to die."

"Oh really," said Kurt. "And why was that?"

"Because killing Lacey was, for me, like killing Primo was for Ringo. It started me thinking. I'd been watching the world change after the Catalyst. I'd been seeing humanity's primitive violence becoming less necessary. I'd been seeing people caring more for themselves, each other, and the world. I'd been seeing people becoming more one with the spirit. But until killing Lacey, I'd been able to keep the professional detachment that had kept me sane for so many years. Killing Lacey caused a crack in that detachment that got bigger over time.

"I became ashamed of my life. I became ashamed of the immeasurable pain I had caused in the name of 'helping the world'. What a crock of shit! For the most part, all I was helping was a deranged little man with a deluded sense of what was right and what was needed to keep the rich and powerful rich and powerful!

"I became ashamed of the life of humanity. I became ashamed of the immeasurable devastation done in the name of patriotism and, even worse, in the many names of the spirit! What another crock of shit! Again, for the most part, all that the pawns, soldiers, and minions of the world were helping were other deranged little men with deluded senses of what was right and what was needed to keep the rich and powerful rich and powerful!" As Lena was talking, she got up and started pacing agitatedly, like something was bothering her.

"I tried to do what I could to make up for my past life. I nurtured the faith that had lain dormant in me for most of my life, at least since I poisoned my father. I spent time communing with the spirit and, even despite my dreadful past, began getting a glimmer of what being at one with the spirit means. I worked behind the scenes to support the Socio movement, with considerable success, I might add. I'm feeling that I may have made up for myself in at least a small way. But I have two things remaining to do."

Chapter 51
(The End)

As Lena was finishing up, she walked behind Kurt and put her hand on his shoulder. "I'm sorry, dear," she said. "This won't hurt at all."

"What? Wait!" Kurt said. But it was too late. Lena covered his nose and mouth with an ether-soaked rag. *Poetic justice*, she thought for a moment, *finishing Kurt's life in a way that might have been used in the days he seemed to yearn for.* She kept the ether soaked rag over his nose and mouth. Kurt's body convulsed and then he was gone. *What a pity*, she thought for a moment, *an ether overdose in someone so young, and with such apparent promise, too.* A single tear rolled down her cheek. She was getting soft in her old age.

Lena laid Kurt down on the couch, covered him with a blanket as though he might have come to his secret hideaway for a nap, wrapped his now lifeless fingers around the ether bottle, put the rag in his other hand, and pushed it up near his face. Investigators would find another partly empty ether bottle under Kurt's bathroom sink, pushed back behind some cleaning supplies. Lena knew that because she had put it there. She wasn't sure why she was being so careful, this time, though, because this time was different. *Old habits die hard*, she guessed.

Lena reached into her bag again and this time drew out a short sword. The almost-cylindrical handle was about a third the length of the whole sword. The blade was thin but exceptionally hard, scalpel-sharp, and came to a triangular shaped tip. "No, this one's not for you, Kurt, my dear," she said. She got down on her knees and grasped the handle, blade toward her, and placed the tip of the sword at her abdomen. Without even a whimper and with brutal surgical precision, she made two deep incisions that not even the most discriminating Samurai warrior would have found wanting. She held her position, despite her entrails in her lap, and hoped for a moment that this might in some small way restore honor to her people. By people, she meant the people of the world and their sons and their daughters and their child-mates and their husbands and their wives and their life partners and their mothers and their fathers and their past and present and future friends.

Finally, Lena had a wish she had never had before. She wished for the friend who was supposed to come and complete her ceremony for her, ending her suffering by beheading her with the same brutal surgical precision she had used. But no such friend came. There was no such friend and there never was. *Poetic justice*, she thought for a moment. And then she was gone.

Chapter 52
(The Beginning)

Jennifer was getting a little worried. It wasn't like Kurt to ignore her nets and he had now ignored at least two, maybe three. And now, on top of that, he was very late. He was normally never this late without at least letting her know. *This is not fair*, Jennifer thought to herself with a mixture of disappointment and annoyance. *The one time I have the most wonderful news for him and I can't contact him.* She tried to net Kurt one more time. But he did not respond – he couldn't.

And time ticked on...